Sensual NIGHTS

USA TODAY BESTSELLING AUTHOR

PJ FIALA

*To the lovely women of my reader group, PJ Fiala's Road Queens,
who help me out with names of characters, places, and businesses,
thank you. I appreciate and adore you.*

Characters
The Road Queens who named Characters:
Brenda Borders Rudell *named Dr. Walker Borders*
Angela M. Carter *named Dustin Carter - Military Information
Thief*
Geraldine Collins-Ellis *named Neil Ellis - Condo Buyer*
Alison Conville *named Brian Terry - Layton Terry's grandfather*
Sharon R. Cowan *name Asa - Owner of Unit 1*
Karen Cranford LeBeau *named Burke Thompson - Mason's
brother*
Terri DeMario *- Mitch DeMario - (Security Specialist former
Marine, Hero in book 6)*
Kimie Dougherty *named Lieutenant Ethan Dougherty*
Gayle Lazur *named Kaysen - Employee at the Sandbar*
Carolyn Wolf McCutcheon *named Bear - Mason's friend*
Elinda Moody *named Erin Moody - Police officer with Blossom
Springs*
Tina Susedik *named Heidi - Carley's German Sheppard*
Michelle Terry *named Layton Terry - Buyer at the condos*
Jo West *named Trey Fielding - Police Chief of Blossom Springs*

Dana Zamora *named Jonathan Roberts - Neighbor to Douglas Sanders*

To my family, my greatest blessing and unwavering support system. Your love, encouragement, and sacrifices have made this dream possible.
And to my husband and best friend, Gene—thank you for standing beside me every step of the way. Your belief in me, your patience, and your love are the foundation of everything I do. Words will never be enough to express how much you mean to me, but I will spend my life showing you.

***

To our veterans and all those currently serving in the armed forces, police, fire departments, and as EMTs—your courage, dedication, and sacrifices do not go unnoticed. Thank you for your unwavering commitment to protecting and serving. It is with heartfelt gratitude and deep respect that I honor you here. You are the true heroes, and your contributions inspire every word on these pages.

Map of
Blossom Springs
Drawn by PJ Fiala

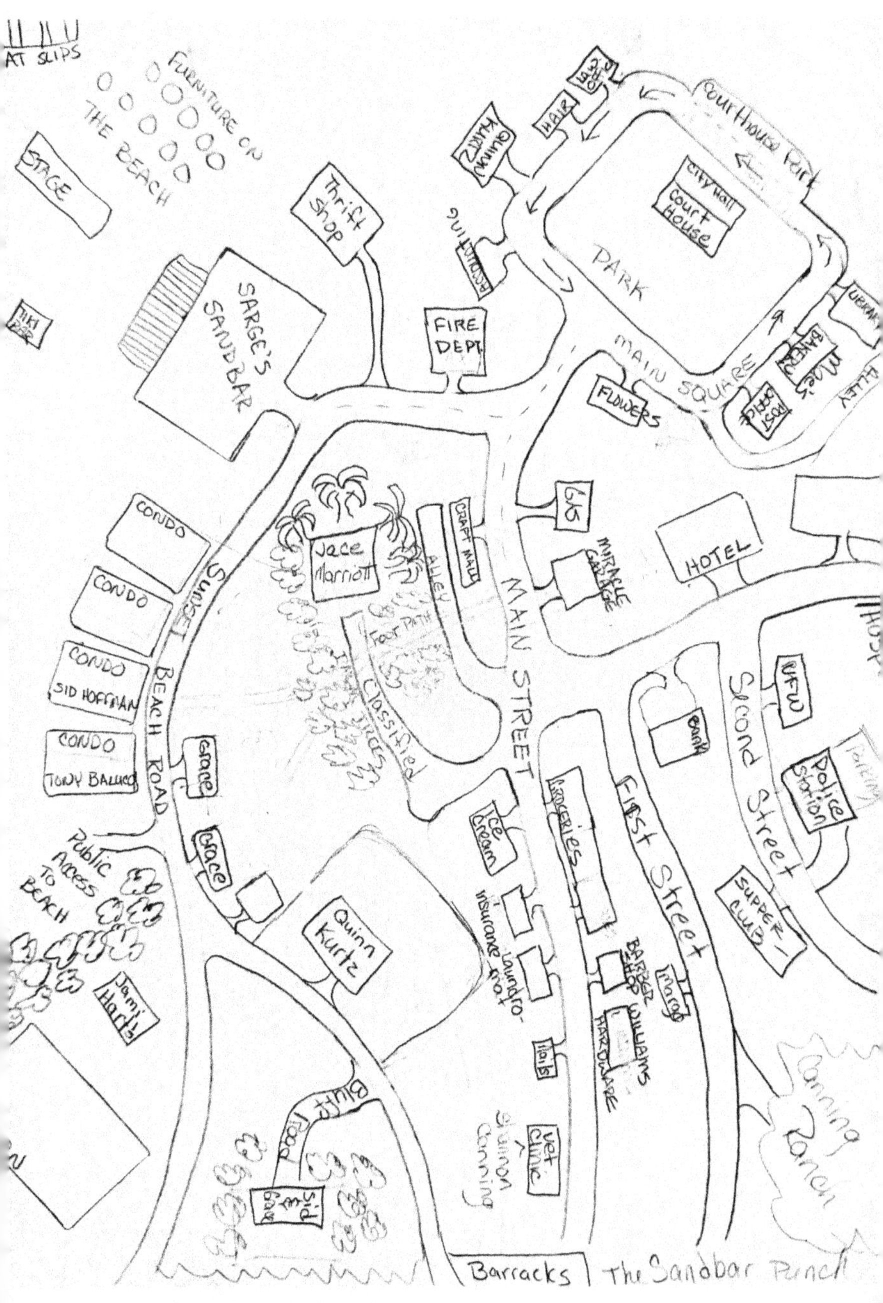

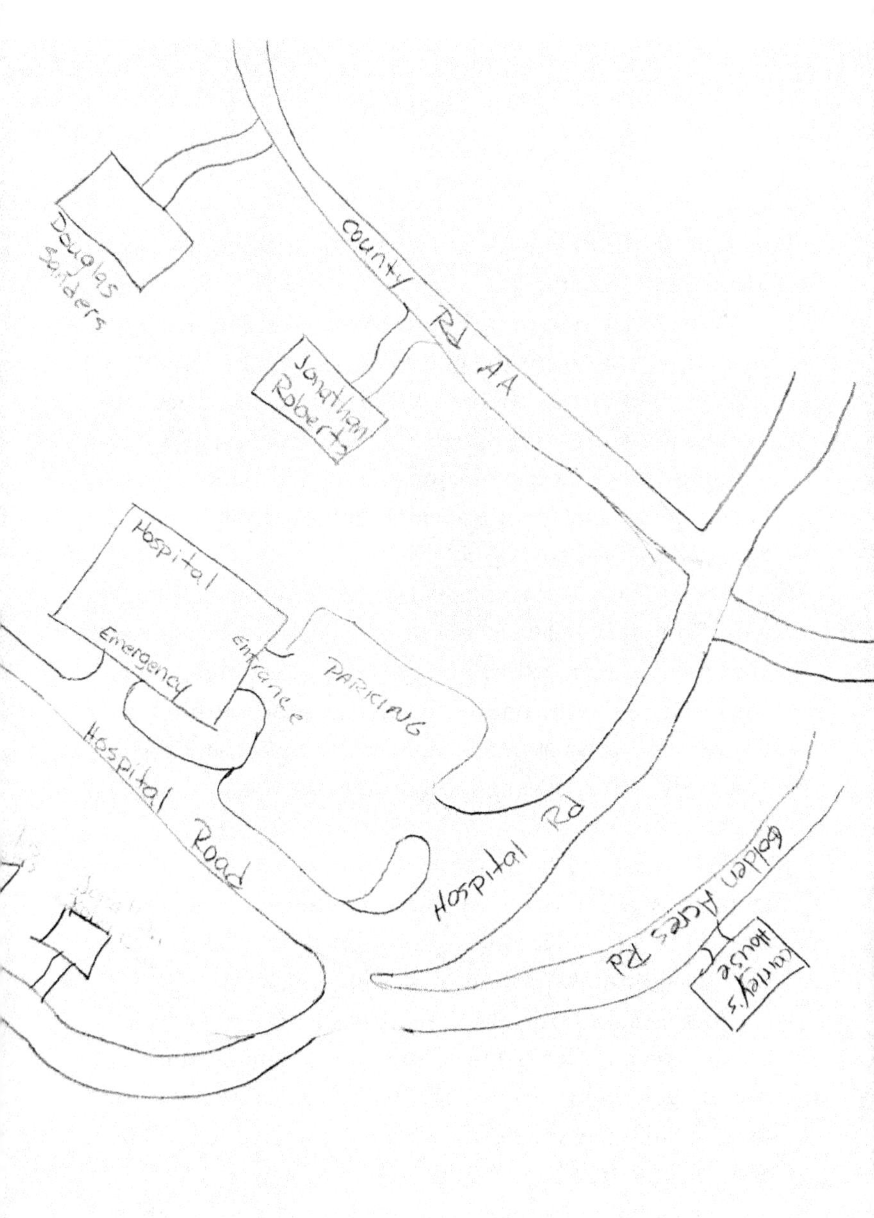

Douglas Sanders
Jonathan Roberts
County Rd AA
Hospital
Emergency
entrance
PARKING
Hospital Road
Hospital Rd
Golden Acres Rd
Kinney's House

DESCRIPTION

In a town built on second chances, will love be their ultimate redemption?

Mason Thompson, a former Army surgeon, has spent years trying to escape the ghosts of his past. Battling PTSD and haunted by the lives he couldn't save, he's taken refuge behind the bar at Jace Marriott's pub in Blossom Springs. Tending drinks keeps him busy, but deep down, Mason knows he's capable of so much more—even if he's too broken to believe it.

Carley Page is starting over, leaving heartbreak behind and diving into a new career at her sister's real estate firm. Her first big job is selling luxury condos for veterans, a task she's excited to take on. But when a routine showing turns dangerous, Carley stumbles upon a deadly secret hidden in one of the units, placing her in the crosshairs of a ruthless enemy.

When Carley's life is suddenly at risk, Mason's protective instincts kick in. The chemistry between them is undeniable, but with danger lurking in every shadow, Mason will have to confront his own fears to keep her safe.

As the stakes rise and the passion between them deepens, Mason and Carley find themselves bound by more than just danger. Can they overcome their fears and scars to find love, or will the dangers of their pasts threaten to tear them apart for good?

Sensual Nights is a thrilling, small-town romantic suspense filled with sizzling chemistry, heart-stopping action, and the promise of redemption. From USA Today bestselling author PJ Fiala, this is a story of love, danger, and second chances in Blossom Springs.

***

USA Today bestselling author PJ Fiala brings you the Servicemen of Blossom Springs series—heroes willing to sacrifice everything in service to their country, and for the men and women they love. A novel with no cliffhanger, no cheating, and a happily-ever-after guaranteed.

Looking for stories filled with heart-pounding suspense, steamy romance, and unforgettable characters? Sign up for my newsletter and get a **FREE book** to dive into right away!

It's easy: 1 Sign up below. 2 Confirm your email (we like to keep things legit and bot-free 😉). 3 Start enjoying your free read and exclusive updates, sneak peeks, and special offers!

📚 Love awaits—don't miss your chance to join the adventure! ✨

https://www.pjfiala.com/subscribe/

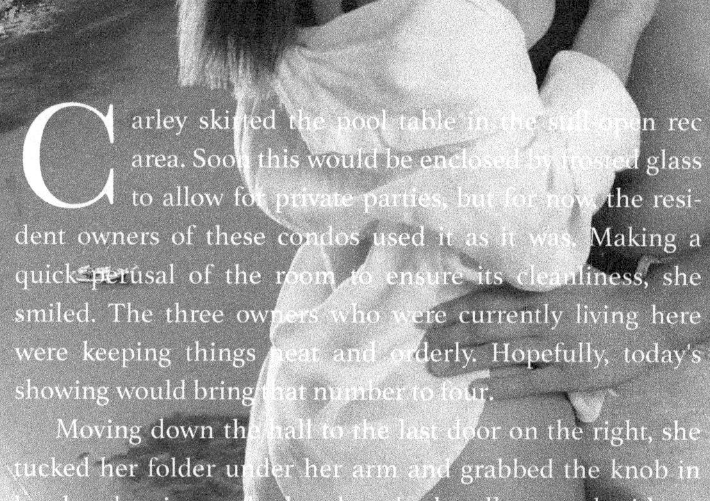

1

———

arley skirted the pool table in the still open rec area. Soon this would be enclosed by frosted glass to allow for private parties, but for now, the resident owners of these condos used it as it was. Making a quick perusal of the room to ensure its cleanliness, she smiled. The three owners who were currently living here were keeping things neat and orderly. Hopefully, today's showing would bring that number to four.

Moving down the hall to the last door on the right, she tucked her folder under her arm and grabbed the knob in her hand to insert the key, but the handle turned without resistance. Her brows furrowed, and her skin heated. She pushed the door open slowly and tentatively stepped inside. She quickly flipped on the lights and listened carefully as she perused the living room.

"Hello?" she called out. Hesitating to move in further, she listened for any sound. Sucking in a deep breath, she moved further into the unit, halted, pulled a door stopper from her bag, and pushed it under the open door. Better to be safe than sorry.

Satisfied she was alone in the unit, she checked the living room closet, happy the contractors had finished the carpeting inside, but the doors still needed to be installed. Moving to the primary bedroom, she checked the closet, which had also been completed, but the carpeting looked pressed down as if something heavy had been sitting on it. She bent and brushed her hand over it to raise the pile once more. Standing back, she was happy with the results and started to move on.

As she turned, something glinted in the light, and she twisted to peer into the closet once more. Kneeling down for a closer look, she swiped her fingers over the shiny object. It was cool and firm and not supposed to be there. She pulled at it, finding it difficult to pull up. It had tucked itself between the trim and the carpet. Wiggling it free, she pulled it from its hiding place and stared at a medallion of some sort. It was heavy-duty in appearance, though it had scratches and marks on it. She tucked it into her purse and moved into the second bedroom to check that the closet in there had been finished as well.

A door closing in the building startled her and she stepped from the bedroom into the living room.

Not seeing anyone around she moved into the hall and called out, "Hello?"

No one responded. A tingling slid down her spine, and the hair on the back of her neck stood up. She inhaled deeply. Her fingers shook slightly as she hugged her folder to her chest and focused on evening out her breathing. Feeling a bit sheepish for being scared, she took a deep breath and once again called out, "Hello. Is anyone here?"

She'd sold three units here in the Barracks Condominiums. It was likely one of the owners coming home. Nothing untoward had ever happened here, and her imagination was certainly flying high today. She blamed her sister, Margo, for watching a scary movie with her this week. She shook her head slightly, took a calming breath, and stepped toward the door when the outside door opened. She held her breath... until she saw him.

Mason Thompson. His very presence was comforting and scary all at once. She'd been watching him as he worked at the Sandbar. He was good with customers, and he could make the best Sandbar Punch, which was some concoction of rum and juices. When he'd called her to see this condo, butterflies took flight in her tummy. The idea of being alone with him was both exciting and nerve-wracking. They'd seen each other in passing but had never spent time together talking. That was mostly because she was so enamored by him that she couldn't take the next step and talk to him. She reasoned it away with excuses such as he was working, or he wasn't interested, or she'd had a couple of drinks and would make a fool of herself. And the biggest excuse was she wasn't interested in a relationship right now. She'd just gotten out of a long-term relationship that had tired her out to the point of near mental exhaustion.

He had also given no indication he was even remotely interested in her, much to her disappointment. But she was the realtor in charge of selling these condos for the developer, Quinn Kurtz, and, therefore, the person he'd call. She pretended otherwise a couple of times this morning, imagining he'd actually wanted to spend time with her (oh, happy day!). However, she was't interested in a relationship right now and needed to keep telling herself that.

He meandered closer to her, and she closed the distance to meet him halfway. She held out her hand as she neared and smiled, though the butterflies in her tummy threatened to lift her off the ground.

"Hi, Mason. My name is Carley Page, from Price Realty."

He wrapped his strong fingers around her hand, which seemed ridiculously small compared to his.

"I'm aware of who you are. It's nice to formally meet you."

The deep timbre of his voice sent chills skittering all through her body. The warmth and firmness of his handshake was imprinted on her brain. She'd never forget it. Yes, she was just that sad.

There was a brief, awkward silence as she caught herself staring at him. After all, his dark hair, broad shoulders, and very presence were unforgettable.

She slightly shook her head and cleared her throat. "I'm sorry. Please come in and see the condo first, then we can take a look at the amenities."

He nodded but stood still. A brief hesitation fell between them, then he held his hand out to her, palm up, and she realized he was waiting for her to enter the condo. Her cheeks burned at her foolishness, and her knees shook slightly as she forced herself to walk.

Suppressing the urge to shake her head as she stepped into the unit, she stood against the wall to her left as he entered the condo and passed by her. He wore some delicious aftershave, and the aroma quickly filled the room.

Inhaling deeply, she pushed herself off the wall as he looked around the room. She silently chastised herself for being a silly foolish woman and quickly switched into professional mode.

"As you can see, this is the living room, with an open view of the kitchen. The appliances are stainless steel, the flooring is tile planking."

Mason stepped into the kitchen area and looked around. He didn't open the cupboards or drawers. Her brows pulled together slightly, and she smiled. "You're welcome to open the drawers and cabinets."

He grinned, and their eyes met. His eyes were brown, and he had thick dark lashes framing them. Her heartbeat increased, and she felt the heat rise up her body. He looked away, and it felt like the sun had set. He opened a couple of cabinets and the refrigerator, then turned and nodded.

She stepped into the primary bedroom first and he followed. "This room has its own bathroom just around the corner to your right. The closet is here to my left. The doors will be installed this week."

She saw him grin and take a quick look inside before he turned to her and nodded. "Okay. I'll take it."

"But...you...will? I didn't show you the amenities."

He laughed, and the air whooshed from her lungs. He was stunning.

"It will suit my needs perfectly. It's larger than the apartment I'm living in now. It's close to work. It's quiet here and everything is new. I know Quinn Kurtz and the quality of work he does. What's not to like about it?"

She chuckled. "I agree with you, but it's a large purchase."

"I'm good."

She blinked and then smiled. This was the easiest sale ever! "Okay. How about if we walk down to the community area? There's a table we can use, and I can get the offer written up."

He nodded. "After you."

She moved toward the door to the hall. As she stepped into the hall, something moved in her peripheral vision, and she squealed.

Mason stepped out behind her. "What's wrong?"

"I just saw someone run out the door."

Mason took off at a run and pulled the main door open easily. She hurried down the hall, pulling her phone from her slacks pocket in case she had to call the police. As she arrived at the door, Mason stepped inside and they nearly collided.

"Was there someone here?"

"I saw him run into the woods at the back."

"Oh, my God." Her knees shook in earnest, and her breaths came in spurts.

"Where would he have been hiding? These condos are all locked, aren't they?"

She swallowed, "They are, but the upstairs isn't quite finished and some of the units don't have doors yet." She paused remembering the door to his unit had been unlocked. She'd need to tell Quinn to remind his guys to lock up behind themselves.

His voice was low and soft. "Let's go and take a look upstairs."

2

Mason led the way up the stairs in case someone was still up there. He was happy he was buying a lower unit; he wouldn't want to do these stairs all the time. Climbing stairs was not hard, but he preferred his workout to be more of an organized effort. Weights, then rowing, then a swim. On alternate days, a nice long jog.

He stepped onto the landing of the second level and stood to the left to wait for Carley. He was torn between asking her to stay downstairs or letting her follow him. What if someone was still down there? What if they were still up here? He'd been away from his military training for a few years now, it was supposed to be ingrained in him so tightly that it'd never leave. Where was it now?

Carley stepped into the upstairs entryway. He watched her swallow and hug her folder to her chest. His heart felt heavy for her fear. He'd never know what it was like to be a woman and feel afraid that someone would harm her. He'd been in combat; he'd hurt people as part of his job, and he'd lost people. Some of them due to acts of war and some because he couldn't save them. Those were the people who haunted him at night. The blank stares of men and women on his operating table after they'd passed on, because he couldn't save them. If he'd been a better surgeon, he could have helped them.

She turned her face up to him, her smile faltered slightly, and he sucked in a breath. He had been told he could look menacing at times. It was usually when he thought of his past life as an Army doctor. He had so much darkness in his past and he carried the weight with him every day.

He took a deep breath and let it out. "Do you want to wait here while I check the units?" he asked.

Her smile grew and she shook her head. "No, I can check them out."

"How about we go together?"

Carley's face brightened and the fear that had been so present a moment ago seemed to vanish. He smiled at this beautiful woman. He'd watched her at the Sandbar when she came with her sister, Margo, who was married to his boss, Jace Marriott. She stuck with the women she came with and refused the many passes from the single men who frequented the bar, especially on music nights. She also seemed sad and that's what he first noticed about her. This little dark-haired beauty seemed sad. As sad as he was. His soul called to her, but she didn't answer the call. She never made an effort to come and chat with him. He couldn't take the step of talking to her though, after all, he was a bartender and as damaged as anyone could be. What on earth would she want with him?

He placed his hand lightly on the small of her back and

matched her steps as they moved to the first unit on the left. The door was locked, and that seemed to put her at ease. She unlocked it, and they stepped inside together. Mason quickly did a recon, checking all points where someone could hide. When he returned to the living room from the bedroom, Carley stood facing him.

She smiled sweetly. "You've done that before."

He shrugged and felt his cheeks heat. "Military training."

She nodded. They stared at each other for a moment before she took a deep breath. "On to the next?"

"Sure."

He followed her out the door, waited as she locked it, and stepped to the next unit. Within a few moments, they'd checked all the units and found no evidence that anyone had been there.

She shook her head. "I feel silly."

"You shouldn't. I saw someone running away from here, so there was someone inside."

She shrugged. "I don't know how he would have gotten in. The front door was locked when I got here."

"There's many ways he could have gotten in. Let Quinn know. Maybe he needs to get the security cameras up and running sooner rather than later."

"I will, for sure." She took another deep breath and tucked a soft, wayward strand of hair behind her ear, and the motion mesmerized him. Her fingers were slender and looked smooth. Her hair was dark and wavy, and it shined where the light hit it. She was petite in build, but her straight posture made her look taller than she was, which he guessed at about five foot three.

She nodded. "Okay. Let's head downstairs and I'll write up your offer."

"After you."

He followed her down the stairs, watching her hair as it moved with each step. He swallowed the lump in his throat and took a deep breath. Carley moved to the first small round table near the wall and sat down. She pulled a long sheet of paper from her folder and removed a pen from her purse.

He sat across from her quietly, watching her hand as she neatly printed on the Offer to Purchase form. His name, the address of the condo, and the basic information she easily recalled from memory without having to look things up. That impressed him. It didn't hurt that he liked looking at her, so there was that.

As she worked on the Offer, she halted and turned her eyes up to his. "What price do you want to offer?"

His brows furrowed. "The asking price."

Her head cocked to the right. "Okay."

"Is that wrong?"

Her smile was beautiful as it grew. Her eyes twinkled. "I don't want to tell you what to do, but most people would offer less and see if it works."

"How much less?"

She took a breath. "I'm not supposed to help you with that part. After all, I work for Quinn. I'll only say some people have offered five thousand less and have been happy with the acceptance. You didn't hear it from me."

His heartbeat quickened as he watched her. She was helping him. "Okay. Let's go five thousand less than asking."

Her smile grew and she nodded. "Perfect."

Her hand flew across the page until she got to the bottom. "What will you put down for earnest money?"

He shrugged. "Five thousand seems like a good number."

She grinned, and he saw the hint of a dimple on her left cheek. She wrote the earnest money in the blank spot, then looked up at him again.

"When would you like to close?"

He shrugged. "It seems nearly ready, just closet doors. I'd like to move in right away if possible. I have to give thirty days' notice on my apartment, but that gives me time to move slowly and get someone to clean my apartment."

"Will your bank be able to get the funds available to you right away?"

"I'm not getting a mortgage. I have the money. I only need to go to the bank and withdraw it."

Her eyes widened but she wrote a date on the blank line. "I have to give the title company a week. Will that work?"

"A week is good."

She finished up the offer and tucked her paperwork away. "I need to head back to the office and enter this on the computer. I'll email it to you through a document signing company we use. You'll electronically sign it, and I'll send it to Quinn. I'm sure he'll be happy to accept it."

She stood and picked up her folder. She held out her hand and he happily wrapped his fingers around it. It was smooth and warm, and felt wonderful in his hand.

"Thank you, Mason. It was nice seeing you."

"Thank you, Carley. It was nice seeing you, too. Next time you come to the Sandbar, please stop and say hi. I'll buy you a drink."

That smile. Wow, it shined brighter than the biggest star. "Thank you. That's lovely."

They exited the building, and he decided to step up and be chivalrous. He moved toward her car and opened the door for her. Her eyes met his and held for a few moments and he felt his stomach twist. He shouldn't be encouraging her. He really had nothing much to offer her, as damaged as he felt.

She gracefully seated herself in her car, and he closed the door. He moved to his truck, got inside, and blew out a deep breath. Whew, that was...something.

3

Carley eagerly typed out the email to Mason with a grin on her face. She'd woken this morning to the news from Quinn that he had accepted Mason's offer.

Mason, attached, please find your accepted offer on the condo at The Barracks. You can officially begin packing your things as you'll be moving soon. By which, I mean Quinn says he knows you and has given permission for you to begin moving in tomorrow if you like. Please let me know when I can meet you and give you the keys. Carley.

She re-read her email to make sure nothing was misspelled. Happy with the tone of the email, she clicked "send".

Her belly rolled in excitement for Mason's new purchase, and it was the fourth sale for her in the past month. She was finally making the money she'd always known she was capable of, without the financial drain of her loser ex. New town, new home, new job and not just any job either. She was running her own real estate business. Thanks, of course, to her sister. Margo coached her along, shared her knowledge of all things real estate, and helped her find new business. At Margo and Jace's wedding, Margo made it a point to introduce her to all her clients and prospective clients. Few people got a start like she had, and she wasn't going to blow it.

Taking a deep breath, she got up, poured herself another cup of coffee, and strode down the hallway to her bedroom to get ready for the day. The weather was warm today; a typical day in central Florida.

"And I love it," she said out loud for no one to hear.

That was the only hard part about living here. She'd bought Margo's big house at a steal when Margo moved in with Jace. Then she'd gotten an incredible deal on Price Real Estate from Margo. Basically, both she and her sister were ready to move on from their former lives, and the timing had worked out for each of them. But she was a tad lonely here. Maybe she should get a dog. A dog would be some company and provide a bit of security, not that her security system was bad. She'd think more about the dog idea today.

After showering and dressing, she gathered her laptop case, files, and her cute little black purse with the chain strap and locked her doors. Jumping in her SUV, she turned the air conditioning on high as she slowly pulled from her garage. Today was a good day!

She grinned all the way to the office. The music on the radio matched her mood.

Stepping into the office, she greeted Addison, her assistant. Addison came with the office and she knew more about the entire business than she did, but she was learning.

"Good morning, Addison. How are you this morning?"

"I'm great. How are you?"

"I'm great too. It's going to be a good day. I sold another condo last night."

"Fantastic! You also have two messages from potential sellers on your voicemail. I forwarded them when I got in this morning. And the title company has a couple of questions about the Juno deal."

"I'll take care of that first. Thank you."

She moved into her new office, Margo's old one, and smiled as she once again had that feeling of disbelief that this was all hers.

Sitting at her desk, she booted up her laptop. Then she listened to her voice messages as her computer woke up.

She returned the title company's call and set up appointments for the two potential sellers for today. She stood to leave for the first appointment when she saw Mason's email slip into her inbox.

Her belly shivered as she saw his name. Quickly clicking to open it, she read his reply.

Thank you so much. I appreciate it and I'll make sure to thank Quinn when I see him. I'm working from noon till around nine tonight. I can meet you before I go in, or it will have to be tomorrow. Mason.

She was on her way to her first appointment now and didn't know how long it would take. She felt slightly deflated thinking she'd have to wait until tomorrow.

She stepped out of her office and stopped at Addison's desk. "I'm off to meet Douglas Sanders. I put his address in the computer. I'm trying to meet up with Mason Thompson, the buyer of condo number four, to give him the keys, but I don't know when that will be."

"I can keep the keys here and he can stop in."

"No!" She softened her tone. "That's okay, I'd like to do it in person."

Addison's smile spread across her face. "Is that the big

guy who tends bar at the Sandbar? The handsome one with the killer smile?"

Carley's heart beat a bit faster. She smiled and Addison grinned.

"Yes. That's him. Do you know him?"

Addison shrugged. "Only in passing. I've seen him at the Sandbar, and my girlfriends and I like to watch him work. His hands are...efficient."

A little jealousy bug crawled up Carley's back and her shoulders stiffened. "Yes. That's my estimation as well."

Addison's brows rose into her bangs, but she didn't say anything further. Carley started toward the door. "I'll be back later in the day."

Carley finished her appointment with Douglas Sanders, catching herself a few times looking at her watch. He had a lovely home, though it was dated. But it seemed lately potential buyers didn't care as much if they got a good deal. Douglas Sanders was eager to sell, as he was moving this week to be closer to his children on the Space Coast and didn't want an empty house for too long. His eagerness was good news for her and any buyers she showed the property to.

As soon as noon came and went, she knew she wouldn't be able to meet up with Mason today. She swallowed the lump in her throat and drove to her second appointment.

Finishing up that appointment, she headed back to the office and cheerfully announced to Addison that she'd earned two more listings. She laid the paperwork on Addison's desk to enter into the system and schedule the photographer for photos.

She returned phone calls and checked her email, then decided to be brave and go to the Sandbar to give Mason his keys. She'd hoped to meet him privately, but honestly, what was that going to do for either of them? She shook her head at her silliness and chided herself for not being professional.

She parked at the Sandbar, took a deep breath, and let it out in a whoosh. She shook her head at her nervousness. After all, her sister and brother-in-law owned the Sandbar, and she was welcome any day and any time. It was natural for her to stop here. She was the one making it more than it was.

She entered the Sandbar, and her eyes landed on Mason immediately. He was chatting with patrons at the bar, two women and a man. The women were laughing overly loud and cocking their heads in the most flirtatious way. It rankled her, even though it shouldn't. After all, she sold him a condo and that was the extent of their relationship. He was the buyer, and she was the realtor.

But she liked his quiet strength. He didn't need to fill any conversational void with idle chatter. He could be quiet and present but not busy. He was different from anyone she'd ever known.

He stopped chatting with the customers at the bar and his eyes landed on hers. They held for a few moments, then he smiled, and her heart thudded in her chest.

4

Out of the corner of his eye, he saw Carley walk in and stop near the door. The girls at the bar were being flirty and it made him feel skeezy when women he didn't know came on so strong. The chick in the tight white sweater was laying it on thick. From his peripheral vision, he saw her pull her sweater down to show more cleavage. She was on the hunt, but he wasn't interested in being her prey, or anyone's.

When Carley didn't approach the bar, he looked up to see what she was doing and saw she was watching. From her vantage point, it probably looked like he enjoyed the attention, but it was his job. The longer they stayed at the bar, the more money they brought in. He wasn't stupid; he understood capitalism as well as the next person. Since Jace had given him a chance to work here, he wasn't going to let him down by chasing paying customers out the door.

When his eyes met hers, he couldn't look away. She was a gorgeous woman. The first time she'd come into the bar, he noticed her. It was right after her sister's husband passed away. He didn't know anything about her, but he knew she was pretty and she always had a smile on her face. She took a few steps toward the bar, and he set a napkin on the top, in front of an empty stool away from the flirty girl.

He smiled at her, and she smiled back. It lit up her face, and it took his breath away.

"What can I get you?" he asked, though his voice cracked.

Her smile grew, "I'd love an iced tea, please."

"Not a Sandbar Punch?"

She laughed and it sounded like music. "It's the middle of the day and I still have work to do."

"Fair enough."

He turned and poured her an iced tea, setting it on the napkin. She pulled a twenty-dollar bill from her purse, and he shook his head. "It's on me."

"You don't have to do that."

"I'm aware."

She smiled again, took a sip of her tea, and licked her lips. He watched every movement.

"Oh." She pulled her purse onto her lap. It was a ridiculously small purse with a chain for a strap. He figured she could fit her phone in it, and nothing else. But it worked for her. She pulled something small from inside, and her brows pinched together. She dropped it back into her purse and pulled out a set of keys. "I thought I'd bring these to you in case you want to get an early start on moving tomorrow."

She held the keys up, and he gently took them from her hand, brushing his fingers against hers. Her skin was warm and soft, though they barely touched, he could tell. Her eyes dropped to their hands, then flicked up to his eyes.

Her eyes were an incredible blue. Framed in dark lashes with a head of long dark hair, she was a picture.

"Thank you," he finally answered.

He took a deep breath as he pocketed the keys, and she nervously played with the little chain strap from her bag.

The door opened and Quinn Kurtz entered with a flourish. "There he is."

Mason saw Quinn staring at him, and he felt heat climb up his body. He didn't relish extra attention. "Hi, Quinn. Thank you for letting me move in early. Carley just brought me the keys."

Quinn stopped next to Carley, and she reached over and shook his hand. "Congratulations on selling another condo, Carley. You're killing it there."

"Thank you for trusting me to sell them for you. They really do sell themselves, or maybe I shouldn't say that."

Quinn laughed. "I'm sure you have a lot to do with them selling."

Her cheeks turned pink, and it was stunning on her.

"You want a beer, Quinn?"

"Yes, please."

Quinn sat next to Carley, and Mason hustled to pull a beer from the cooler. He set the beer and a clean mug on a napkin in front of Quinn.

Carley turned to Quinn. "Yesterday when we were at the condo, I saw a man running from inside. Mason saw him too. I don't know how he got in, but maybe one of the workers left a door open. Also, when I got to the condo Mason bought, the door was unlocked."

Mason tilted his head slightly and a chill ran down his back. "You didn't say anything about that."

"I thought I was being paranoid. After all, the carpenters had been installing the carpeting in the closets. I assumed they left the door unlocked."

Quinn's brows bunched. "Did you see the man enough to be able to identify him?"

"No."

Mason cleared his throat. "I saw him too. I chased him out of the building and saw him run into the woods. We checked the other units..." His eyes met Carley's. "It didn't appear that anything was damaged. We locked up afterwards."

Quinn nodded. "Thank you for telling me. I think I'll have the security system installed tomorrow. Since residents are living there now and someone managed to get in, I'd rather take care of that right away."

Carley nodded and Mason responded. "Thank you, that's wonderful. I'm not worried about me, but Carley shouldn't be showing the place alone if there's someone causing trouble there."

"I agree," Quinn responded.

Jace came out of the back office and greeted his friend and sister-in-law. "Carley, Margo will be pissed if you don't go back and say hello while you're here."

Carley laughed. "I will."

Jace sat on the other side of Quinn, and Carley finished her tea. "I'll go see Margo now. Let me know if I can help you with anything, Mason."

His cheeks warmed, and so did the tips of his ears. Jace gave him a funny look; one side of his smile ticked up higher than the other, and Mason busied himself washing glasses.

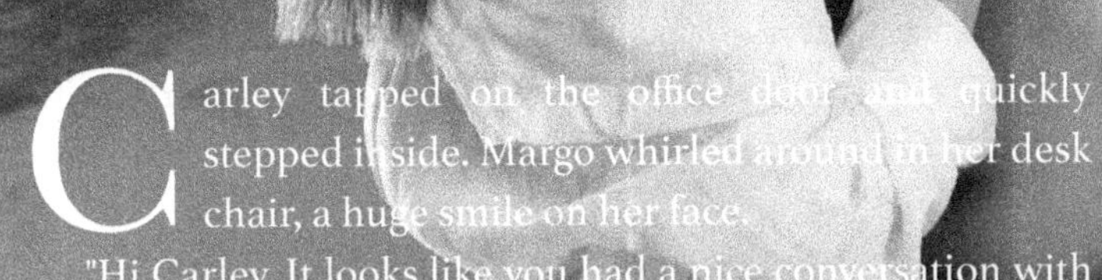

arley tapped on the office door and quickly stepped inside. Margo whirled around in her desk chair, a huge smile on her face.

"Hi Carley. It looks like you had a nice conversation with Mason out there."

"Are you spying on me?"

Margo grinned and pointed to the three monitors on the wall. "I saw you. Not spying on you."

Margo stood and wrapped her in a hug. Carley hugged her little sister in return, enjoying the feel of her sister's warm embrace. She closed her eyes and let Margo's warmth seep in.

Margo stepped back and looked into her eyes. "Is everything okay with you?" She saw concern in her sister's eyes and that bothered her.

"Yes, everything is fine. I sold another condo and brought Mason his keys. Quinn's letting him move in before closing so he can get out of his apartment."

"Aw, that's so sweet of Quinn. He's a good person."

"He is." Carley stared at her sister, whose appearance

had changed tremendously in the past few months and it was for the better. She smiled at Margo and took a deep breath. "You look happy, Margo. I hadn't realized how much your appearance has changed in the past few months. You looked tired and kind of sad before. Now, you look bright, vibrant and ten years younger. Marriage agrees with you."

Margo laughed. "This marriage agrees with me. The last one, not so much."

"True. I should have clarified."

Margo sat in Jace's vacated chair and motioned to hers. "Take a seat and tell me what's going on."

Carley sat and faced her sister. "I'm selling these condos easily. I've gotten two new listings this week and I love selling real estate." She took a deep breath. "I'll never be able to thank you enough for the opportunities you've given me. I appreciate it more than you know."

Margo's smile was infectious. It lit up her entire face. "I knew you could do it. You're my sister and I want only the best for you. I'd have done anything to get you away from that loser, Don, you were living with."

Carley nodded her head. "I'm embarrassed about the years I spent with him. I must not have had any self-esteem."

Margo laughed. "Well, the same could be said of me. So, here's to new beginnings and bright futures." They high-fived in the absence of drinks to cheer with.

She sat back and listened as Margo told her about the new ideas she had for the Sandbar. She was excited and alive when she spoke of her husband, Jace, and the plans they had. Carley was happy for her sister and brother-in-law, but a little hole of sadness built in her heart and felt like a weight.

A half-hour later, Carley's phone and watch chimed. She

glanced at her wrist and saw a text from a potential buyer. She grinned.

"I have someone else interested in looking at the condos. We'll have to push Quinn along to get the rest of them built, the way they're selling."

Margo laughed. "Good for both of you. And I might add, success looks good on you."

Carley laughed. "It sure does feel good."

Carley stood and Margo jumped from her chair and wrapped her in a warm hug once more. Carley was the older sister of the two, yet she was seeking comfort from her younger sister. What did that make her? She should always be the strong one. At least that's what their father would have said.

Her eyes filled with moisture, and she blinked rapidly to dry them. Margo pulled back, and the beautiful smile she'd had on her face only moments ago faded. "What's wrong, Carley?"

"Nothing."

"Bullshit."

"It's...nothing."

"I said. Bullshit."

Margo's eyes bore into hers and held.

Carley took a deep breath and let it out slowly. "It's stupid."

"I bet it isn't."

"It is."

"Well, I could use a little stupid right now. Then we'll both chuckle about it and move on with our day."

Carley rolled her head on her shoulders and huffed out another breath. "I guess I'm feeling a little lonely. Or something. I don't know. I'm more successful than I've ever been.

I have a fantastic home. My own business. I don't know what's wrong with me. See, stupid."

Margo pulled her in for another hug. "Aww, honey. It's not stupid. I used to say the same thing to myself when Logan was on a trip, and I rattled around the house alone. I thought I was the most pathetic creature on earth."

"You did?"

"I did."

"You never said anything."

Margo chuckled. "Of course not. I didn't want anyone else to think I was pathetic."

"Oh." Carley grinned. "I get it. I didn't want to tell you just now either."

"Right?"

Margo took her hands and squeezed them in hers. "I love you. Holly and Josseline love you. Jace loves you. Our friends love you. You're amazing, beautiful, smart and successful. Girl, you've got it going on."

That started a giggle that bubbled into laughter, and the two of them stood in the middle of Margo's office and laughed.

Jace walked in. "What's so funny?"

Carley pulled back, still laughing. "I'm successful."

Jace looked between the two women. "Why is that funny?"

"It isn't. Not really," she replied.

Jace's brows pinched together. He glanced at his wife, and she started laughing again. "I'll tell you later, honey," she managed to get out between breaths.

Jace shook his head in a "women" sort of way, snagged a notebook from his desktop, and slipped out the door without another word.

Carley watched him leave, then turned to her sister

and they both laughed again. There wasn't anything funny at all, but boy did it feel good to laugh. That's most likely what she'd been missing lately. She'd been too busy to do much in a social way and she missed the fun and banter she had with her sister and their friends, Grace and Hanna.

"I could really use a ladies' night out. How does that sound?"

"That sounds great to me. I could use one too. We've been working our tails off. How about Thursday night? We have a great band playing here and Jace is taking off to go to the Legion with Sid and Quinn. It'll be perfect."

She felt the invisible weight she'd created over the past few weeks, lift from her shoulders. "That sounds like a great idea. Thank you."

She turned to leave when Margo said, "Wear something sexy for Mason."

She froze but didn't turn around because her cheeks felt as though they were on fire.

Deciding instead to leave, she strode past the bar where the flirty girls were still perched on their stools, and Sid and Quinn still sat at the other end of the bar. She turned her head to see Mason watching her, and her cheeks burned a little hotter. She smiled and waved at him before hurrying out the door.

Once she was outside, she sucked in the fresh air and hurried to her SUV. There was a note on the windshield in scribbled handwriting.

"You have something that doesn't belong to you, and I want it back."

Her heart hammered in her chest, and she looked around in all directions to see if someone was watching her. Scared, she hurriedly got into her car and locked all the doors. Thinking better of it, she twisted in her seat to make sure no one was in the backseat.

Her hands shook and her breathing came in spurts. She wasn't sure what she should do, so she pulled from her parking spot, watching her mirror to see if anyone followed her. As she turned onto Sunset Beach Road, she sucked in a deep breath and let it out slowly. She should have gone back inside.

A car pulled out behind her, and she watched as it followed her around the corner and onto Main Street. She watched the car in her mirror, nearly hitting the sidewalk. Pulling her SUV back onto the street, she slowed down. Quickly turning left, she entered the grocery store parking lot. She drove around the perimeter, the car followed her partway, then pulled into a parking spot. Carley blew out a breath and circled the lot until she came to the exit once more. She turned right onto Main Street and drove down Hospital Drive, which took her past the hospital and out of town to her house.

The car didn't follow her, and she shook her head at her paranoia. She pulled into her garage, watching both ends of the street to make sure no one had followed her. Quickly closing the door, she heaved out a sigh of relief. She reached over to the passenger seat to grab her purse and saw the note.

Dread filled her once more.

6

Mason grinned as he hauled his first box down the corridor to his brand-new condo. Brand-new aptly described this place. He'd literally be the first person to live here and that was a thrill by itself. To be out of that tiny, noisy apartment, well, that just made his heart sing. The neighbors were loud and always propped the security door open. He'd asked them nicely a few times to stop doing that. After all, it wasn't a security door if anyone could walk in. They laughed at him and called him a scaredy cat. He didn't have the energy to explain to idiots what a security door meant. After talking to the office about it and nothing changed, so he'd set his sights on leaving that place. Finally, he was doing it.

He inserted his key, then stopped, checked that the door was locked, satisfied it was, then turned the key and pushed the door open. Carley had said the door was unlocked when she'd arrived a couple of days ago to show him the place.

He set his box on the island between the kitchen and living room area and turned to retrieve a few more boxes from his truck. He'd do his main furniture moving this weekend. Marco from the Sandbar offered to help him out, as did Quinn and Jace. He'd be out of his little apartment in no time.

He carried another box of kitchen items down the hall-way, grinning as he walked. This move felt good to him. It felt positive, and he was finally ready. When he'd first come to Blossom Springs, it was an escape. A chance to get away from the haunted faces he still saw at night. Those he couldn't save. Maybe that's why that apartment always felt so oppressive. He'd selected it without looking at any others. He just needed a place to sleep. He then found out Jace was only hiring veterans and that seemed a good place to start for employment. Working as a bartender was so far removed from his days as a surgeon.

He set his box on the counter and turned to retrieve the final four boxes he'd brought with him today. Stepping outside, he sucked in the warm, humid air and closed his eyes. Gawd, he loved it here. The warmth seeped into his skin. Even though he sweated a lot, it felt good.

Pulling a box of dishes from the back of his truck, he hustled to the door, unlocked it with his key, and pulled it open awkwardly while juggling his box. He stepped inside and started down the hall, but the door didn't close. He waited for the 'thunk' it made, but it didn't. He turned to see a head disappear outside. Someone was out there.

Setting the box on the floor, he hustled to the still-open door and pushed it open. The hand of a man was holding the door, but he'd managed to open it easily. He glanced down at the short man with a slim build, scruff on his chin, and hair that needed to be combed. Disheveled. That's how he'd describe him. The man's grayish eyes rounded as his head tilted up to stare into his.

"What can I help you with?" Mason asked, never looking away from the scrawny man.

"No..noth...nothing." He shuddered.

"You live here?"

"No. no." He shook his head.

"Okay. Well, you need to live here to be in here. Or know someone who lives here. Do you know someone who lives here?"

The man shook his head and moved back a step. His hands fidgeted together, and in a split second, he turned and ran toward Main Street. Mason watched him run. It wasn't the same man he'd chased the other day. That man was larger in build and neater in appearance. The little bit of it he'd seen anyway.

Sucking in a deep breath, Mason pushed the door closed tightly, checked that it was locked, and once he was satisfied it was, he turned to finish taking his dishes into his new condo.

Setting the box on the counter, he turned and surveyed his new place. His furniture would look great here. He shook his head to remove the suspicious feelings that invaded his mind after seeing that man try to enter his new sanctuary. He wasn't going to tolerate stuff like that here. The other owners needed to know that about him right away. Hopefully, he'd meet them sooner rather than later, and they could come to a consensus about safety.

He heard the entry door open and pushed himself off the counter he leaned on and stalked toward the door. His irritation rose to a new level for today and if that scrawny little bast...he halted when he saw Carley standing near the pool table with a clean-cut younger man. He looked recently discharged from the military. His high and tight still evident, though beginning to grow out. His posture was ramrod straight, and as Carley explained the common area, he stood nearly at attention.

Carley turned and saw him in the hall. Her smile grew as her eyes landed on his.

"Hi, Mason. This is Neil Ellis. He's looking at a place here. Neil, this is Mason Thompson. He's moving in today!"

Neil stepped forward and held his hand out. Mason planted his hand against Neil's and shook. "It's nice to meet you, Neil. I'm looking forward to living here."

"I am as well, Sir."

Mason shook his head. "Mason."

"Yes, sir...Mason."

He grinned at Neil. His eyes slid over to Carley's, and he smiled at her. "I just have a couple more boxes to carry in; then I'm off to work."

Neil stepped toward the door. "Let me help you."

He seemed nervous and Mason remembered those days when he was first out of the military. It was scary in so many ways. After years of someone barking at you and telling you what and when to do something, it was unnerving to be able to make your own decisions and choices. Or even to have to make your own decisions and choices.

Mason grinned at Carley. "I don't mean to hijack your showing."

She laughed. "Don't worry. Actually, if we all pitch in, you'll be moved in before you know it."

He nodded and held his hand out for her to precede him. Besides, he didn't mind watching her walk.

His eyes reluctantly drifted from her fabulous ass to the surrounding area as he stepped outside. He was looking for both the scrawny man and the man he'd seen the other day. For some reason, they were keenly interested in the Barracks. But why?

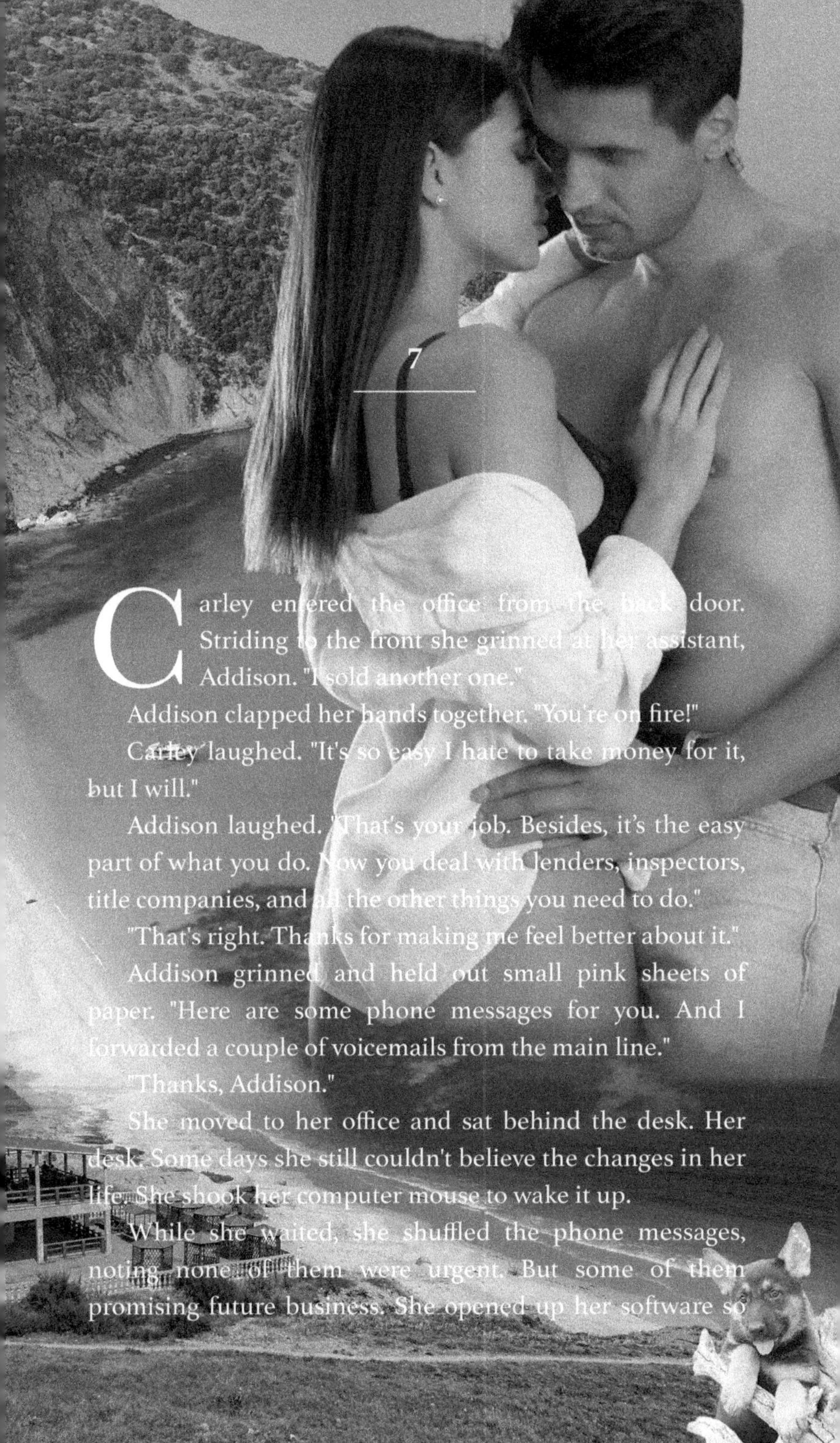

7

Carley entered the office from the back door. Striding to the front she grinned at her assistant, Addison. "I sold another one."

Addison clapped her hands together. "You're on fire!"

Carley laughed. "It's so easy I hate to take money for it, but I will."

Addison laughed. "That's your job. Besides, it's the easy part of what you do. Now you deal with lenders, inspectors, title companies, and all the other things you need to do."

"That's right. Thanks for making me feel better about it."

Addison grinned and held out small pink sheets of paper. "Here are some phone messages for you. And I forwarded a couple of voicemails from the main line."

"Thanks, Addison."

She moved to her office and sat behind the desk. Her desk. Some days she still couldn't believe the changes in her life. She shook her computer mouse to wake it up.

While she waited, she shuffled the phone messages, noting none of them were urgent. But some of them promising future business. She opened up her software so she could type in the offer for Neil. He seemed nice, but a tad nervous. Mason seemed to warm to him instantly, and that made her feel good. Mason was a good man.

She shook her head, why did it take so long to finally find a good man? Not that they were an item. Not at all, but she'd married early in life, then divorced. That was a rocky relationship at its best. She remembered her mom asking her not to marry him. At the time, Carley thought she could change him. His volatile temper would simmer if she gave him enough love, right? After a few years of being afraid, she got the courage to divorce him. After that, she worried, fearing he would stalk her or show up one day and hurt her. Then, he died in a car accident, and as terrible as it seemed, she was relieved for the first time in years that she didn't have to worry about him.

Later on, she met Don. His personality was the polar opposite. Laid back, not volatile, no temper. If she'd only stepped back and listened to her family, especially Margo. Laid back turned to lazy. He couldn't keep a job, and he had little ambition to find another one. She worked so hard, putting in as much overtime as she could to pay the bills. Then she'd come home from work and have to work more. Don didn't even so much as cook. He sat on his butt in a chair all day playing video games. It was maddening. She huffed out a breath and shook her head. For all she knew, Mason wasn't who she thought he was either. She had terrible taste in men.

Her software loaded, but before she started the offer, she began typing out an email to Izzy Payton, the daughter of the town's former flower shop owners, who'd recently moved to town and took over running the Flower Shoppe. Like everything else here in town, or the majority of the businesses were simply named. The Bookkeepers was just that...bookkeepers. It was something she'd always grinned about when she came here. Sid's place used to be called The Garage. He kept some of the name when he bought it and renamed it Miracle Garage.

She'd always joked with Margo about the name of this office, Price Realty. "Why didn't you name it Real Estate, so the other businesses don't feel bad?"

Margo always laughed, "It doesn't have the same ring to it."

She reread her email to make sure there weren't any mistakes in it. *Hey Izzy, it's Carley again. I need to order another mirror and floral arrangement. This one is for four weeks from now. Around the fifteenth of July.*

She'd been ordering these mirrors for her new clients' house warmings, which Izzy made at the shop. They had a small floral display in the corner and some sort of a homey type saying on the mirror. "Home Sweet Home", "There's No Place Like Home", and "Home is Where the Heart Is" were the most common. Once in a while, Izzy got tired of the same old thing and switched it up. She never specified and let Izzy's creative imagination flow.

After finishing her email, her stomach growled. Checking the time on her computer, her eyes rounded. She hadn't been paying attention, and it was after lunchtime. As soon as that thought floated through her head, the thought to eat at the Sandbar entered, and with a smile on her face, she rose from her chair and called out to Addison, "I'm heading out for lunch. See you later."

Addison waved. "Have fun."

If that girl only knew some of the thoughts that floated through her head lately, she'd be embarrassed. They both would. Lately, she couldn't stop thinking about Mason.

She hustled out the back door and jumped in her SUV.

As she backed from her parking spot, she saw a scrawny man peering around the corner watching her. The fine hairs stood on the back of her neck, and her breathing came in short bursts as she drove away.

He didn't look familiar at all, and the goosebumps that rose on her arms prickled. He moved his body to stand in the road behind her as she drove away. Her mind began racing; he was watching her. He knew her car. He...she froze. Was he the one who wrote the note? All she had was that old scratched-up medallion she'd picked up between the carpeting and the wall at the condos. It could be his. And why was she keeping it? She had intended to give it to Quinn so he could ask his employees if it belonged to any of them. She'd forgotten about it. It seemed so insignificant. But now she was afraid to stop and offer it to him. And why was he in Mason's condo? And how did he get the door unlocked? Her mind raced with questions about what she should do.

She turned left onto Sunset Beach Road and then right into the Sandbar parking lot. The lot was full, so it took a minute to find a spot to park. She grimaced a bit as she parked at the far end of the lot near the woods. Maybe she'd be lucky enough to walk out with someone. She'd ask Jace to walk her out. He'd certainly do that for her. Though it made her feel like a wimp.

Better a wimp than dead. Or worse. Wait, was there worse? She could think of some unpleasant things that would certainly feel worse than death. A shiver ran down her back, and she chastised herself for thinking such morose thoughts.

She huffed out a deep breath, looked around her SUV, and found it clear, then jumped out, locked the door, and hustled into the Sandbar. Yeah, she was a wimp all right.

The inside was relatively quiet, considering all the cars outside, but then again, most folks liked sitting upstairs on the deck that overlooked the water. The rest sat outside near the beach. The only time the inside was super busy was when it rained.

She glanced at the bar, and there he was. He stood tall and proud; his broad shoulders pulled back. It was easy to see he was former military. She wondered what branch of the military he had been in. She'd have to ask him. She strode to the bar and sat on a stool near the end.

Mason greeted her with a sexy smile. "Hey, there. Nice to see you."

She smiled brightly; it was impossible not to. "Hi, there. I thought I'd stop by and see what the lunch special was and how you faired with your move."

He chuckled. "I only moved a few boxes in for today. Tomorrow, Jace, Quinn, and Marco..." He waved his thumb over his shoulder toward the kitchen. Marco was the chef there "will be bringing in the furniture. I'll then have to find some time to unpack."

"I can help with that." She froze after she'd said it. She'd blurted it out without thinking and now she felt like a fool. Her cheeks burned.

He grinned. "I'd like that actually."

He would? It took her a moment to realize what he said. "You would?"

His grin hitched up on one side and damn if that wasn't sexy. "Yeah."

She swallowed as he set an iced tea in front of her. She hadn't even ordered yet, he remembered. "Okay. Do you want me to come over tomorrow? While you are moving furniture in, I can be unpacking dishes and things."

Mason nodded. "That would be great. Then I can actually sleep there tomorrow and get some sort of order. I may even be able to find things and make breakfast."

She chuckled. "I'll do my best to organize things for you, so you can make breakfast."

"Thank you, Carley. That's very kind of you. I appreciate it."

She smiled and stared into his brown eyes. "I get lonely at home by myself, so I'm happy to help you out and do something that makes me feel useful."

Mason stopped wiping the bar and stared at her for a long moment. It felt like minutes. Long minutes. "You should always feel useful. And you should never feel lonely."

Her heart raced in her chest as his eyes bore into hers. Then someone from the other end of the bar called Mason away and she felt lost. Lonely all over again. That was stupid though, right?

8

Mason dipped his head and wiped the sweat from his forehead on his forearm. He and Marco were carrying his sofa down the hallway to his new condo. The Florida heat had him sweating as soon as he walked outside this morning to put things in his truck. He'd need a couple of showers today. The humidity was high and the temperature was higher. He should have looked at the weather before choosing to move today. He didn't even give the weather a second thought though, he wanted out of that apartment.

Marco stopped at the door to his condo. "We're going to have to tip it up on the side."

"Okay."

They worked together to tip the back of the sofa down and eased it through the door. Once inside, Marco grunted. "Where do you want it?"

"I don't know. What about against that wall?"

"You won't see out the patio doors that way."

Carley stepped inside, staring at the two of them holding a sofa, both of them sweating profusely. "If I may offer some assistance here, I'd say place the sofa right here." She moved to a spot on the floor. "That way, you can see out the patio doors and see into the kitchen. If you put your television above the fireplace, you can see both easily."

He grinned and looked at Marco. "You heard the lady."

They moved around and placed the sofa where Carley suggested and set it down. Both men mopped the sweat from their faces again as Carley set two grocery bags on the counter.

He glanced at the bags, "What's in there?"

"Cleaning supplies in this one." She pointed to the bag on the right. "Lunch in this one." She motioned to the bag on the left.

"You didn't have to buy cleaning supplies or lunch."

She smiled and he stood staring at her like a fool.

She began removing items from the cleaning supply bag. "I know. I wanted to. Now, finish getting your stuff in here so the air conditioning can catch up without the doors open."

He turned and followed directions without another comment. Marco followed him down the hallway, chuckling.

"What are you laughing at?"

"Nothing."

He glanced back at his friend. "What?"

"You just jumped when she said jump."

"She brought food."

Marco laughed full-on at that. "Right."

They stepped outside to see Quinn and Jace pulling up in Quinn's truck with his bed, dresser, and night tables. He felt grateful for the help.

Quinn stepped out of his truck and looked into the box

of Mason's truck. "Should we finish this one first, then start on mine?"

Mason nodded. "Sounds good."

He jumped into the back of his truck and scooted his end tables to the tailgate. Quinn and Jace grabbed those, so he moved his coffee table to the end. After jumping down, he grabbed one side and Marco grabbed the other. They handily carried the table down the hall.

"You've got some nice furniture, Mason."

He shrugged. "My mom helped me pick it out." He grinned. "She has good taste."

Marco laughed. "Does she like Carley?"

He felt his cheeks burn. "They haven't met."

Marco grinned as they entered his condo. Carley was instructing Quinn and Jace on furniture placement, so he and Marco waited patiently for their turn.

After Quinn and Jace left for the next load, Carley grinned at him. "How about in front of the sofa?"

"You got it."

They set the coffee table down and turned to leave again. But a fantastic aroma caught his attention, and he stopped. "What's that smell?"

Carley laughed. "It's lasagna."

"You made lasagna?"

"I did. I know it seems silly to eat something so warm and heavy in this weather, but when you're working so hard you need to keep your strength up."

"Thank you so much for doing that."

She looked up into his eyes, and he stared into hers. The blue of her eyes was the prettiest blue he'd ever seen. She smiled then, and his heart swelled. She was not only beautiful, but she was also thoughtful, kind, and she smiled more than any woman he'd ever known. Not like the flirty women at the Sandbar. Carley was naturally happy. Her sister, Margo, was also that way. It had taken some time to get used to being around happy people again. His life had been so dark for so long, he didn't know how to behave around people who were just simply happy.

"I wanted to do it. It felt good cooking for someone again. It's been some time. Normally, at home, I don't make big meals for just me."

He sucked in a deep breath as he heard Jace and Quinn coming down the hallway again. He hated to step away, but he did need to get the trucks emptied. "Thank you. I do appreciate all you're doing for me."

She smiled again. "It was my pleasure, really."

He nodded and stepped back. He wanted to kiss her. Badly. He wanted to pull her into his arms and kiss her. But there were people around, and he was likely a smelly mess. Plus, he didn't know if she wanted him to kiss her.

He turned just as Jace entered the condo carrying a box marked "Fragile". Jace grinned at the two of them standing face-to-face. He looked at Carley first, then his eyes slid to Mason's. Mason felt the tips of his ears burn, but he recovered by directing Jace to the coffee table. "If you want to set that box on the table, I'll unpack it later."

Jace chuckled and did as he was asked. After standing he asked, "What are you having to eat?"

"Lasagna."

"Nice." He left the condo without another word and Mason took the opportunity to follow him. As soon as he stepped outside, he saw the rest of his friends lugging his mattress off the truck. He hustled over and helped Quinn carry it inside. Marco and Jace started on the bed frame.

Within an hour, the trucks had been unloaded and the final load from his apartment had been brought back and unloaded. They carried the dining room table and chairs into the condo and Carley laughed. "Just in time. If you're all done, go wash your hands and get ready to eat."

They all did as they were told to do.

Mason was the first to return to the kitchen. Carley was carrying plates to the table, but he gently took them from her hands. A thrill ran up his back as their fingers brushed. "Let me do that."

He set the plates out, noticing an extra plate. He turned and Carley laughed. "Margo's on her way too."

"Okay. That's nice."

Margo entered with a flourish and without knocking. Carley chuckled and shook her head. "This is Mason's home now, Margo."

"I know." She took two steps. "Oh, I should have knocked. I'm sorry, Mason."

He felt his face heat, but he shook his head. "It's no bother. Please come in."

Margo carried a package with her, and she handed it to him with a smile on her face. "This is from Jace and I. Happy housewarming."

"Oh." He had a lump in his throat at all the kindness surrounding him today. "Thank you."

Margo shrugged. "Open it."

Jace stepped from the bathroom and came to stand next to his wife. They watched as he opened his gift. Pulling the lid off the box, he saw that inside lay a metal and wood decoration. It was rustic, manly, and it matched the fireplace mantle perfectly. Margo pointed to the wall next to the fire-place. "I thought it would look nice on that wall."

"How did you know about that wall?"

She shrugged and glanced at Carley. "I know things."

He caught the two women grinning at each other and

knew Carley had a hand in picking this out. His stomach twirled as emotions flooded him. He'd run from his past to find a group of people who were so good and kind that he didn't even think he belonged with them. How lucky he was.

Carley chuckled. "Come and eat before everything cools down."

9

They all sat at the table. Carley sat to Mason's right, her sister on the other side of her. Jace at the other end of the table and Quinn and Marco across the table. They talked about life at the restaurant, which all but she and Quinn had part of. She didn't feel left out at all.

Jace looked at her. "Carley, have you seen that man around anymore?"

Mason froze with a fork of lasagna on the way to his mouth. He set his fork down and turned to her. "What man?"

She swallowed and set her fork on her plate. "When I left the office yesterday, a man was watching me. He stepped out from behind the building next to the office and stared as I pulled out of my parking space. When I drove down the road, he stepped into the road and watched me leave." She took a deep breath. "I was creeped out when I left the Sandbar yesterday afternoon and asked Jace to walk me to my car."

She felt like she'd done something wrong. Mason sat staring at her. "What did he look like?"

She shrugged. "He was kind of scrawny. He wore an older faded blue T-shirt. His jeans had holes in them. His hair was unkempt."

Mason looked at Quinn. "I saw a man who fits that description running from here yesterday."

Quinn's eyebrows shot up. "Was that the same man you saw the day Carley showed you this place?"

Mason shook his head. "No. That man was better groomed and a bit stockier."

Quinn and Mason stared at each other for a few moments. Jace then chimed in. "All of this in a matter of three or four days?"

Mason nodded.

Her stomach twisted. What was going on here? Two men? She finally found her voice. "One of them left a note on my windshield at the Sandbar the other night. It said I had something that belonged to him."

Mason turned his head to her. "Why didn't you say something?"

"I didn't think it was a big deal. I thought it was a prank."

His eyes returned to hers. "Do you have something someone thinks is theirs?"

"I picked up an old medallion or something in your bedroom closet the day I showed this place to you. I dropped it in my purse meaning to give it to Quinn in case one of his guys lost it. I forgot about it."

Mason looked across the table to Jace. He nodded. "I can look back on the security cameras to see who put the note on your windshield. Can you remember the day?"

She felt all eyes on her and she wanted to fall through the floor. She felt like a little girl who'd done something wrong. "It was the night before last."

Margo reached over and placed her hand on top of

Carley's. Her sister squeezed her hand. "Oh, honey. You should have said something."

"I didn't want to make a fuss."

Margo squeezed her hand again, and she squeezed back. Jace nodded. "As soon as I get back to the Sandbar, I'll look at the security footage."

Her cheeks felt hot, and her throat was dry. "Thank you."

Margo moved the conversation on to talk of the town council vote coming up soon, and Carley was grateful the attention wasn't focused on her anymore.

Mason resumed eating, but he was quiet. Quinn changed the topic once more. "The director of the hospital in Tampa called me to ask if we'd consider starting a counseling center on site."

Jace stopped eating and asked. "For who?"

"Veterans."

She saw Mason stiffen as his eyes focused on his plate. She got the feeling this wasn't a subject he was interested in. Maybe it brought up bad memories. She'd seen him have a panic attack at the bar one day. Jace coached him through it. Everyone else who worked at the Sandbar picked up as though nothing was happening as Jace helped Mason through his attack. There were probably many others who could use that help. She was afraid to say it though. Mason didn't seem to be comfortable with the discussion and she searched her brain to come up with a change of subject that wouldn't seem so contrived. Luckily Margo gave her the opening.

"Carley is selling these condos almost faster than you can build them, Quinn."

Quinn laughed. "I know. I've told Jared he may have to work longer hours to stay ahead of Carley."

The mood lightened, and Mason finished eating his

lasagna. Carley stood and began clearing the plates. Margo helped her. Once they were in the kitchen loading the dishwasher, Margo whispered to her, "Are you alright?"

"Yes. Why would you ask?"

"It seemed tense there for a minute."

"I noticed Mason was tense about the conversation surrounding the counseling."

"Why would that make you tense?"

She looked into her sister's eyes and softly said, "I like him."

"Of course, he's very ni..." Margo's eyes rounded, and her brows shot up behind her bangs. "Ohh."

"Anyway. It doesn't really matter. I don't think he feels the same way."

"I think he does."

"Why do you think that?"

Margo took a breath to start to explain, but Mason stepped into the kitchen with more dirty plates. "The lasagna was great, Carley. Thank you for feeding all of us. But I should be the one feeding all of you."

Carley's chest heated as she turned to take the plates from Mason. "You can do it next time."

He shook his head. "I'm not moving any time soon."

She laughed. "Okay. Then, you can host a party or something once we get everything organized."

Margo turned to stare at her, and she realized what she'd said. *Once WE get everything organized.* As if she were living here too. As if she was part pf this.

Mason chuckled. "That sounds good. We'll do that."

He said *we'll*. But before she could say anything, he turned and left the kitchen. Margo had a sassy grin on her face as she put the plates in the dishwasher, and Carley felt...how did she feel? Happy. Flustered. Yes, the word was flustered. She wasn't sure she was even ready for a relationship. She started to tell Margo that, but her sister, ever so astute, whispered, "I think he does feel the same way as you do. Good for you."

Carley swallowed a lump in her throat. "I don't know if I'm ready for something like a relationship again."

Margo laughed out loud, and Carley glanced into the dining room to see if anyone looked their way. None of them did. Margo then replied. "When I met Jace, no one was less ready for a relationship than I was. No one. Look at us now."

"Yeah."

10

Everyone had left except for Carley, who still bustled about the kitchen, putting dishes away and unpacking boxes filled with other kitchen items. She hummed while she worked. It was cute. Mason stepped into the kitchen and watched her for a moment. "Do you mind if I run and take a shower?"

She stopped and stared at him. Her lips turned up into a smile. "Of course not. I'm almost finished with the kitchen. I hope you're okay with where I put everything."

"Thanks." He grinned. "I'm fine with where you put things. I dislike doing that stuff, so I appreciate all you're doing."

Her smile grew and she cocked her head slightly. That was cute too.

He hustled to the bedroom and found his suitcases where he'd packed his clothes. He pulled a clean T-shirt, sweatpants, and clean underwear from inside and slipped into the bathroom in his bedroom. He turned on the shower and rummaged through the boxes on the floor for a towel, soap, and shampoo.

He made quick work of his shower, but what he wouldn't have given to stand under the warm spray of water for a lot longer. He'd been sweaty all day. This felt like a little slice of heaven.

He quickly dressed and exited his bedroom to find Carley wiping the counter off. Her sweet derriere pointed in his direction, and he obliged himself and watched it move back and forth as her arm swiped across the counter. She stood and turned, noticed him watching her, and their eyes locked.

He saw her cheeks turn an adorable shade of pink. He moved toward her slowly. It was as if there was a magnetic pull. It felt natural to move toward her.

He stopped in front of her, and they stared at each other for a long time. Just as he bent his head to kiss her lips, her phone rang. He froze, and she huffed out a breath as her shoulders dropped. She pulled her phone from her slacks pocket, and he stepped back. Her hand reached out and took his and held him there.

"Hi, Jace."

She listened and he watched her face.

"Okay. What will you do with it?"

Her eyes looked into his. "Okay, I'll bring it by tomorrow."

She squeezed his hand. "Okay. Thank you. Bye."

She dropped her phone into her pocket and smiled sweetly. "Jace found the video of the man putting the note on my windshield. He's going to take it to the police tomorrow and wants me to bring the note and the medallion to him."

"Okay."

His heartbeat increased, and he pulled her hand, so she stepped into his space. He let go of her hand and slid his arm around her lower back, pulling her in tighter. His other hand slid into her hair at the nape of her neck. He'd wanted to touch her hair since the first time he'd seen her. Her arms slid around his waist, and her face turned up to his.

He lowered his face slowly, just in case she wanted to back out. She didn't. He wasn't about to. His lips touched hers ever-so-slowly. He then pressed his lips to hers. He felt the sizzle of an electric current run down his body, and their lips began moving with each other. Hers were soft and pliable and they felt incredible against his lips. He breathed in her scent as his mouth moved against hers. The silky strands of hair between his fingers felt as he imagined they would, only better. Her body pressed against his as she opened her lips, and he slid his tongue inside to taste her fully. Their tongues slid together, back and forth; a dance perfectly timed by the two of them. It was as if they'd been kissing each other their entire lives, but it was the first time. The first time feeling her body against his. The first time he tasted her. The first time he heard her whimper against his mouth. He tried imprinting it all into his brain because he didn't want to miss a single thing. He didn't want to ever forget how she felt... ever.

He slowly pulled away to allow them both time to catch their breath. Her face remained turned up to his and he stared into her eyes for a long time. His voice was gruff when he finally spoke. "I've dreamed of kissing you since the first time I saw you."

"You have?"

"I have."

She smiled and it was perfection. "I've dreamed of kissing you since then too."

"Then we've both been having great dreams."

She swallowed. "They weren't as good as the real thing."

He filled his lungs with air as he stared into her eyes. His stomach swirled around, and a newfound energy flowed through his body. He'd never felt like this before. He should have at his age. But relationships had never been a thing for him. He focused on his career as an Army surgeon working on an FST, a Forward Surgical Team. They were much like MASH units set up in times of war.

That thought had his head popping back to his reality. He couldn't put her through dealing with his stuff. Panic attacks coming whenever, especially at night. That's when the ghosts of patients from the past haunted him the most.

What kind of life would that be for someone like Carley? She didn't deserve to have to be woken every night with his tossing and turning or yelling out in his sleep. Telling the ghosts to leave him alone. Telling them how sorry he was he couldn't help them. And he was so terribly sorry. He'd gone into medicine to help people, not hurt them. He'd always wanted to help people. He failed at that though, and he paid for it every day of his life.

Carley's head tilted to the right. "Are you still here with me? You seem to have retreated to somewhere else."

He blinked and focused on her. Her pretty face and long dark hair. The beautiful blue of her eyes was crisp and soulful. She stared into his eyes as if she was trying to reach him. She did. If she only knew how much she reached him. But that would have to be the end of it. She didn't deserve him and his shit.

11

Carley stared at Mason for a long time. "Are you alright, Mason? Is anything wrong? Did I do something?"

"No," he interrupted her. "No, you didn't do anything wrong." He rolled his head on his shoulders. "Hey, I'm sorry I kissed you. I shouldn't have done that."

Her heart dropped. He shouldn't have done that? She thought it was fantastic. "Why? Why shouldn't you have done it? I wanted you to kiss me."

She saw him swallow and step back a little, but she reached forward and grabbed his hands in hers. "Why, Mason?"

He swallowed. He tried looking over her head, but she stood on her toes and then he tried looking down and she bent her knees and looked into his eyes from below.

"Tell me."

He hesitated. She could see him struggling. It was clear he wanted to say something but was afraid or nervous about it.

"Is it because you have PTSD?"

His eyes flicked to hers quickly. "How do you know that?"

She let out a little breath. Her fingers squeezed his hands gently just to comfort him. "Mason, my sister is married to Jace Marriott. I know that Jace only hires veterans, and I know that most of the veterans he hires have PTSD or other issues that they've encountered or developed because of their time in the service. I admire Jace for hiring only veterans and I admire you and all of the veterans everywhere who have served to make our lives better. I don't think anything less of you."

She saw him swallow and take a deep breath. "You don't understand, Carley."

"I do understand. I mean maybe not in the way that you've experienced it, but I do understand."

"No, you don't. You don't understand what it's like with me. I have nightmares. I have panic attacks. I freeze up and I never know when it's gonna happen and it's stupid little things that can make... can trigger me."

She took a step toward him, still hanging on to his hands. Oh, she felt so bad for him. No one should feel less than they should, because they dealt with something that others didn't. Certainly not someone who's served their country and has developed PTSD because of the horrible things that they'd seen or in some cases, done.

"Mason, I was in the Sandbar with Margo when you had a panic attack. Jace ran over to help you through it. I actually think it was what made Margo soften to Jace. She thought he was a cad before that, but then she saw how he cared, how he helped you, and she realized he wasn't what she had thought of him at all. Your attack didn't stop me from liking you and it didn't stop me from wanting to get to know you better. It didn't stop me from wanting to kiss you."

He turned his head, removed one of his hands from

hers, and scraped it through his hair. She could tell he was torn. She was too. I mean, how bad was it that he was afraid to even enter a relationship with her? She wasn't gonna back away. How bad could it be? She couldn't think of anything that would be worse than not trying to live your life.

And then she wondered, and her stomach twisted. "Do you just not want to be with me because of, well I mean, I can't even think of what it might be, but maybe you just aren't interested in me at all and you're trying to let me down easy?"

He huffed out a breath. "No, no that's not it at all. I don't even know what to say." He swallowed. "I just...I just don't want to get involved and then have you decide that you just can't deal with me. I think that would be worse than anything. To get deeply involved and find out that I'm so damaged you wouldn't want to be with me. I'm letting you off the hook, so we don't go down that road."

She could have cried. Tears actually formed in her eyes, and she blinked rapidly. She didn't know what he was feeling, but that just hurt.

She swallowed a couple of times to calm herself, sniffed a little bit, then blinked rapidly to try and dry the tears. "Do you think I'm shallow and wouldn't want to be with someone because you have nightmares or issues? Maybe I would be able to help you."

He opened his mouth to say something, but she shook her head. "Maybe I couldn't help you, but do you think I'm perfect? I'm not perfect. Good Lord. I have..." She inhaled, "I have dealt with lazy. I have dealt with abusive. I have dealt with working my fingers to the bone for someone who didn't appreciate anything. That's not to say that I think that you are any of those, but what I am trying to say is that I didn't leave them right away just because they were different or lazy. I probably should have, but I didn't. What I always tried to do was look for the best in them, and if you ask anyone who knows me, they will tell you the same thing."

He looked at her and squared his shoulders. "You see that's the thing. I don't want you to have to deal with or struggle with anything with me because you feel as though you are committed in some way. Do you understand that? Do you understand what I'm saying?"

Well, she couldn't stop them. The tears flowed from her eyes. She swallowed and sniffed a few times. "Well, what I'm saying, Mason Thompson, is that I don't give up, and I think you're worthy. I think you're worth maybe a sleepless night or two. So what? You have panic attacks. Can't we take it slow? Can't we just get to know each other? A few dates? Dinners out? A movie? Go listen to the music when you're not working? Do something to just see if we even like being together? I mean, hell, maybe I won't like you because you can't sing."

"I can sing."

"Well, I don't know that."

"I mean, I don't sing a lot. I'm not a professional."

"Well, I'd like to know that. Sing for me."

He chuckled. "I'm not singing now."

"See maybe you can't. Maybe you snore."

He finally grinned. "Well, I don't snore. At least I don't think so."

"All right, maybe you're a slob."

"I'm not a slob."

She grinned. "Well, I don't know that either. I'm willing to try and find it all out, though. I'm willing to see if we can get along and like spending time together. I'm willing to do that. Are you?"

She saw him swallow. She saw the indecision in his eyes.

and she figured what the hell. She reached up on her toes, and quickly wrapped her arms around his neck. Her hands slid into his hair. His scalp was warm. His shoulders were broad. His body was firm, and she pressed her lips to his.

He stood still for a while, but she kept kissing him. She pressed her breasts into his chest, and his kiss grew firmer, more urgent. She moved her fingers in his hair, massaging his scalp. And then his arms wrapped around her and pulled her tightly to him.

And her heart felt alive.

She felt alive.

She felt alive for the first time in, well it seemed like forever. It seemed like forever.

12

Mason's heart pounded in his chest as he felt Carley's body pressed against his. He really wanted her. He just didn't know if he could handle it if she couldn't deal with him. He'd given up so much in his life for the military, for his career. One of those things was emotional entanglements with anyone.

He'd had women, but no relationships.

This was the first honest-to-goodness time in his life that he wondered if he could make it work. He sure wanted to. He felt differently about Carley. She was, oh, she was something.

She smiled all the time. She was happy. She was smart. She was beautiful. She was a bright ray of sunshine every time she walked into the room. Who wouldn't want someone like that in their life?

She was running her own business. She was self-sufficient. That's what he wanted. That's what he'd always wanted. He didn't realize it till just recently.

He'd woken up this morning excited that he'd be seeing her today. He'd never woken up in the morning excited to be seeing someone. That's really all he needed to know, right? Let the chips fall where they may.

His hand slid down her back. He cupped her ass and squeezed. She felt good in his hands. Like she was born to be there. Her scent was unbelievable. She smelled citrusy and more. Her body pressed into his felt perfect. She was soft in all the right places and firm where it mattered.

His lips moved against hers and he pulled her tighter to him. His cock roared to life.

She whimpered when she felt the hardness pressing into her. Her hands gripped his hair, and she tugged tightly. Dammit, that excited the shit out of him.

He pushed into her and she did it again. She tugged at his hair and fisted her hands in it. He walked her back against the counter and pushed himself into her again.

And she moaned.

He needed to get out of his head is what he needed. She was right. He had to start living a life. What he really needed right now was Carley.

Her hands left his hair. And quickly slid down his body and under his T-shirt. Her hands on his bare skin made that old electric current sizzle right through him.

Her hands were soft. They were smooth as they brushed over his body.

Up his chest.

Her thumbs rolled over his nipples and his breath stopped for a moment.

Then her hands slid to his back and fully embraced him, and his heartbeat increased.

Slowly her hands slid down and tucked into his sweat-pants. His mind damn near went blank.

Her hands smoothed over his ass and pulled him into her tightly.

His breathing came in spurts, and he pulled his lips from hers for a moment. He lay his forehead against hers. "Carley." He swallowed to wet his throat. "If we do this..."

"I want to do this." she huffed.

"It's gonna change everything."

She swallowed. "I hope so."

Did she though? He didn't know if she really knew. He'd killed people. He'd...

Indecision played with his head for a while until her hands slid around to the front of his sweatpants and her fingers wrapped around his cock.

God.

That.

Felt.

Amazing.

He pushed into her a few times. Her hand moved up and down his length and he couldn't think when she did that.

She kissed his collarbone as her hand worked him.

His hands started undoing the button and zipper on her slacks. As soon as he had them open, they slid down her legs easily. They were made from some slippery material, the way they molded around her ass made him stare at her all day. Most of the day.

As good as they made her ass look, she was gonna look better without them.

As if she could hear his thoughts, she stepped out of her pants, continuing to hold his cock in her hand.

Her other hand slipped under and cupped his balls. The air whooshed out of his lungs.

"Carley."

She kissed his collarbone.

"Stop thinking."

"But..."

"Stop thinking."

She slid his sweatpants down his hips. And he slipped her panties over her hips. He lifted her onto the counter and pulled her toward the edge. He was grateful he was tall. He froze though.

"I don't have a condom."

The air whooshed from her lungs. "Shit."

"I think I have one in the bedroom somewhere. It's packed." He swallowed. "Maybe it's still in the nightstand. I didn't unpack the drawers."

"Let's go see." She hopped off the counter.

He moved to the bedroom holding her hand in his. To the right of the bed was one of his bedside tables. He pulled the drawer open. There was a box of condoms at the back of the drawer. He pulled one out and turned with a grin on his face. He held it up between them.

He swallowed, "You sure?"

That smile. That smile that she lit the room up with appeared on her face.

"Yes, I'm sure."

He ripped open the condom. She took it from him and rolled it onto his cock. Well, dammit, that felt good. She fumbled a little bit. Clearly, she wasn't used to doing this. That actually made him happy.

He helped her roll it on the very end. Then he pulled her into his arms and kissed her lips firmly. He walked them the few steps to the bed.

As soon as the back of her knees hit the bed, he gently lay her down. She scooted toward the middle of the bed, and he scooted with her. She wrapped her legs around his waist.

He swallowed as he looked into her eyes. Man, he

dreamed about this. Never, never, ever did he think that dream would come true.

But he dreamed about it.

He positioned his cock at her entrance and slowly slid himself inside.

She huffed out her breath and moaned when he entered her. He closed his eyes for a moment. He wanted to remember how this felt. He wanted to remember everything about this. It may have to sustain him sometime in the future.

He pulled himself out and then slid back in again. The feeling was just as good as the first time. Her body wrapped around him tightly. Her hands gripped his butt and pulled him into her again and again. Her hips rose to meet him at every thrust. The feeling was incredible.

In and out he moved with her. His lips kissed hers. Kissed her cheek, kissed her forehead.

Each time his body moved in and out of hers, the feeling was incredible.

They stared into each other's eyes for a long time as he moved.

Her face was flushed.

He felt himself sweating. The room was warm.

He pushed in again, and again, and again.

Her hands gripped tightly on his ass.

"Mason, I'm going to come."

"Do it," he growled.

"But I want you."

He pushed in two more times, and she cried out.

He watched her face as the pleasure washed over her.

He pushed in a few more times and followed her over the cliff of pleasure.

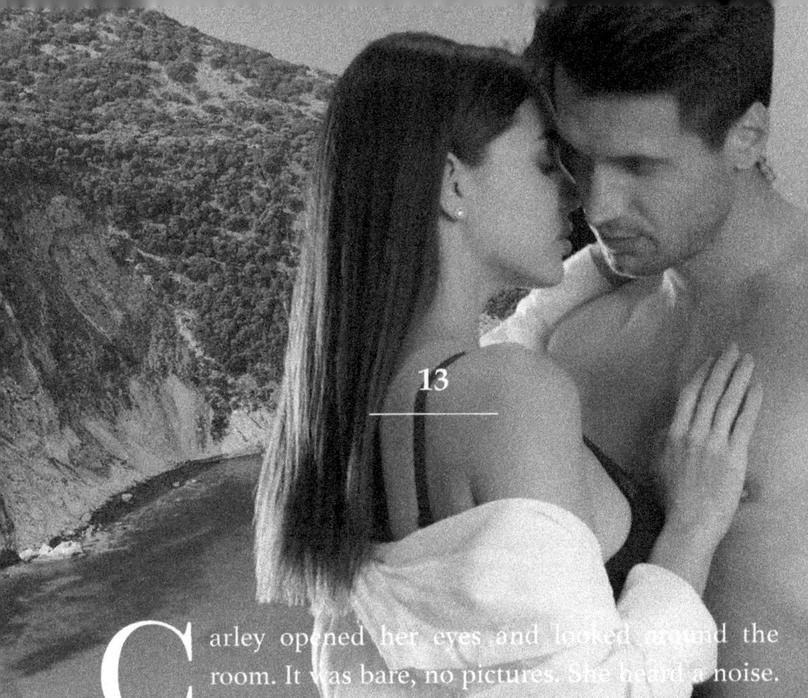

13

arley opened her eyes and looked around the room. It was bare, no pictures. She heard a noise. It sounded like a whimper or a grunt or something, and she froze, she heard it again and rolled over. Mason was sleeping next to her, and he was jerking in his sleep. His feet moved, thrashed. His hands pushed, pushed some invisible thing away on the opposite side of the bed from her.

She softly got out of bed, not sure if she should wake him up or let him finish out his dream or nightmare as it seemed. Wasn't there something about not waking up someone in a sleepwalking state, or...

Suddenly he jerked upright and stared straight ahead across the room. She froze and watched him. He shook his head. With the palms of his hands, he rubbed his eyes, then scraped his hands through his hair and sighed. His head slowly turned to her as she stood watching him. "I told you."

"I wasn't scared. I just wasn't sure what I should do. If I should wake you, or if I should just leave you alone. What should I do if that happens?"

He huffed out his breath. "I don't know. I don't know."

She felt a little embarrassed. She stood there naked. She slid back into the bed, pulled the covers up over her breasts, and faced him. "Have you ever..."

She looked at her fingers and twisted them together, then she looked at Mason. "Have you ever been with someone when you had a nightmare?"

"No."

"Okay. Do you see a counselor?"

"No," he said a little more boldly.

"I'm not trying to make you feel bad and I'm not trying to pry. I'm trying to understand."

"I haven't seen a counselor. I have the names of a couple. I know Jace could help me out with finding someone, too. It's..." He scraped his hands through his hair again.

"It's embarrassing."

"You have nothing to be embarrassed about, Mason. Nothing."

"Says the woman who has nothing wrong with her."

She laughed. "I have plenty of things wrong with me. Plenty."

Their eyes met for a while, then his drifted down the sheet, barely covering her breasts. "Not from where I sit, you don't. You have everything going for you, Carley. You have a business. You're phenomenal. You're smart. You're self-sufficient. I'm a fucking bartender."

"Well, I guess after today, I could say you're a fucking bartender."

She waited. Then she chuckled. "You work in a bar as a bartender, which is not a bad profession. You're good at what you do. I don't see anything wrong. You're gainfully employed. You've got a lot going for you. You paid cash for this condo, for crying out loud. You're alright, Mason. You're doing well."

He huffed out a breath. "I don't know."

She watched him for a while. His shoulders rolled forward, looking dejected. She scooted over toward him, and her hand rubbed his back. "What did you do before you were a bartender, when you were in the military?"

"I was a surgeon."

"A surgeon?"

"Why does that surprise you?"

"It doesn't surprise me as in I don't think that you would be capable of it. It surprises me that you went from surgeon to bartender. I'm trying to understand why."

He huffed out a breath. "Can we not talk about this right now? I'm feeling embarrassed, and that's not exactly the best feeling after having been with someone and having them witness something like my nightmare."

She rubbed his back a little bit more. "You know, it was just a nightmare. People have them all the time."

"Not everyone."

"Some people do."

"Do you?"

"No."

"See, not everyone has them."

She swallowed. "Okay, well you got me there. Not everyone has them and you do. You weren't violent. It's like you were trying to push someone away or something."

"Yeah, that's what I was trying to do."

He got up and stalked to the bathroom.

She watched as he walked. He was incredible. Tall and lean and broad and firm. He was handsome, and he was smart. She didn't know how to help him. She started dressing and devising a plan in her mind. What would she do? She didn't want to divulge any confidences, but she wanted to help him. She really liked him. *Really* liked him.

He came out of the bathroom and stopped in front of her. He reached over, pulled his sweatpants on, and slid the T-shirt over his head.

She didn't know what to say. It was sort of awkward at this moment. What did she say? Thanks for the roll in the hay? She stepped into the kitchen and slipped on her new slacks. They felt wonderful against her skin. She tucked her blouse into her slacks as she moved to the sofa to grab her purse. She didn't want this to be the only time they saw each other. She surely didn't want it to be the last time they slept together. What they had was hot. It was passionate. It was incredible.

As she lifted her purse and slung it over her shoulder, his hands rested on her collarbone from behind. She halted for a moment, and he turned her to face him. She looked up into his eyes.

"I really like you, Mason. Really like you. I've been watching you from afar for a long time, and while I didn't expect us to have sex today, I'm not sorry. I... I guess I don't know what else to say. I don't know what you're looking for. I'm not necessarily looking for anything from you. I just wanted to get to know you better, and things got sexy, and I'm not sorry."

He watched her as she spoke. A grin hitched up on one side of his mouth. He said, "I'm not sorry either and I've been watching you from afar too. I saw you the first time you came in with your sister. I think it was after her husband died, and you all looked..." He swallowed. "Well, I'm gonna take that back. She looked sad. You and your other sisters didn't look as sad, more mad or something. But I remember watching you. You comforted her. You were there for her, and I thought you were incredibly beautiful. I don't want to burden you with anything, Carley. I would like to get to know you better, too. I just want to be honest, I guess. It might not be easy."

She smiled. Her heart felt a little lighter, knowing he wanted to get to know her better, too. "Well, I can't say I'm looking for easy. What I'm looking for is someone I really want to spend time with and someone who really wants to spend time with me. I've never had that ever. I have never had that in my entire life. And you seem kind of lonely, and I am lonely, and I thought maybe our two loveless souls would find each other, and we'd enjoy each other's company."

He kissed her lips softly. "I'd like to get to know you better too. I'm not gonna lie, I liked our afternoon together."

She chuckled. "I did too."

He kissed her one more time and then he pulled her to his body and hugged her tightly.

She wrapped her arms around him and hugged him right back. They stood together for a long time, just holding each other, and that felt better than anything she could ever explain. To just have someone hug you, want to hug you, and want nothing else from you. She hadn't even realized it till right now. What did that say about her?

14

Carley left a while later. He wanted to ask her to stay. They could have watched a movie, but he didn't even have his TV up, and maybe it was just time for them to part for the day. They both had a lot to think about. Maybe tomorrow she would decide he was more bother than he was worth. She didn't really understand what it was like with him. He didn't know how to explain it.

He started unpacking a box in the living room and putting together a shelving unit he had purchased before and never set up. He hung his TV. The whole time he was doing all this, even though he was excited about his new condo and how it was coming together, it felt sort of empty. He liked watching Carley in the kitchen putting things away. She hummed. She seemed happy doing even menial tasks. So much different than what he was. She really was a bright ray of sunshine.

He looked at his phone. It was about eight-fifteen. Normally, he'd be working this time of day, but Jace told him to take the day off. He'd unpack for another hour, and then he'd go to sleep. Actually, what he should do is go in his bathroom and get that organized. He was gonna take a shower every day. Maybe two, the way things were working out here. It was pretty warm and humid in Florida.

He sauntered to his bathroom and began unpacking the boxes. There were only three. Bath towels took up one box. The other two were a scale and his razor, blades, and bandages. The last box held shampoo, shower soap, his brush and comb, a blow dryer, aspirin, and other pain reliever products. He probably could have gotten the last two boxes into one, but he had the boxes and decided to keep them light.

After unpacking his bathroom, he unpacked his clothes. He felt pretty good about his first day at the condo. He never dreamed he and Carley would have had sex and hoped it wouldn't be the last time. Then again, he was apprehensive about getting involved. Tomorrow would be a new day, and he'd see how things were with him and Carley then.

THE NEXT MORNING, MASON WOKE, LOOKED AROUND THE room, and realized he'd slept most of the night. He remembered waking up a couple of times, but he went back to sleep easily. He didn't have the nightmares. He just woke up. His mind thought of Carley every time he woke. He laid back down and closed his eyes and remembered how she felt, how she smelled, how she sounded. He managed to go back to sleep and liked that feeling the most.

He woke, stretched and scratched his chest. Leaving his comfy bed, he strolled into the kitchen and grinned. Carley had made the coffee and set the timer. He looked into each of the cupboards to see where everything was and chuckled.

She had everything so neat and organized. Even his coffee cups were perfectly lined up.

He grabbed his phone, sat on the sofa with his cup of coffee, and texted her.

"Good morning. Thank you so much for organizing my kitchen and making coffee. It was easy for me to find a cup to pour my coffee in this morning. What a nice surprise. Thank you again for all you did yesterday. I really do appreciate it."

He sent it off with a huff wondering if she'd respond right away. He sipped at his coffee, scrolled on his phone looking at the news, and then her text popped up.

"Good morning. I was happy to help you out. I'm available anytime you want some help, and I really did enjoy getting to know you better. I hope to see you soon, Carley."

He stared at the text, "Hope to see you soon."
He responded without giving it a whole lot of thought.

"I have to work tonight until eight. If it's not too late, we could go out for a drink somewhere, or we could just go for a drive, or something else."

He sent it off wondering if that was the right thing to do, and if she said yes, what would they do? No sense in worrying about it all right now. He could always ask Marco where to go. She responded right away.

"Or something else, what does that mean?"

He laughed.

"Yeah, that probably did sound bad."

Another text came in from her before he could even respond.

"I have a showing at the condos at two-thirty and nothing after that. We could do something when you get home. I hear there's a band playing in the park, some local ensemble that's trying to get their name out there, if you're open to it."

He chuckled and his fingers flew across his phone,

"That sounds good. I'll plan for that. See you later, Gator."

She sent back a laughing face emoji. He finished his coffee, took his cup to the kitchen, and washed it. Putting it in the cupboard where Carley had placed it.

He turned to see the stack of empty boxes in his living room and opened the drawers in the kitchen to see where Carley had put the junk drawer. He had a box cutter in there somewhere. Locating it in the third drawer he opened, he set about cutting up the boxes and made a neat stack of cardboard on the floor. On his way out, he'd dump the stack into the recycle bin.

His phone rang. He pulled it from his pocket without looking at it and grinned.

"Good morning, sexy."

A male voice responded. "Okay, good morning. It's Jace."

He could feel his ears burn.

"Sorry, Jace. I thought you were someone else."

"Clearly. I've been called sexy by my wife but never by one of my employees, so I'm not sure how to take that."

Mason nervously laughed. "Sorry, I really did think you

were someone else. I should have looked at my phone before I answered."

"Okay, well anyway, Kaysen can't make it in today, and we have a big truck delivery. I'm not going to be able to relieve you for lunch since I'll be in the storeroom. I just want to give you a heads-up. Might be a busy day today since we're running short-staffed."

Mason nodded. "It's okay, I can even come in early if you need me. I'm just kind of rattling around here anyway. I'm just cutting up boxes. I can come in and unload the truck and maybe leave a bit early tonight."

"That sounds great. I didn't want to ask, but I sure appreciate it. Thanks, Mason."

"You're welcome, Jace. I'll see you in a little bit." He hung up the phone, shook his head, and laughed at himself. He made plans for tonight and that was a first in such a long, long time. It actually felt good to be able to laugh at himself. He hopped in the shower and got ready for work.

15

Carley grinned at her phone and her tears from Mason. Then she tapped her sister's picture and put the call on speaker. The phone rang twice before Margo answered, "Morning, what's going on with you today?"

"I'm wondering if you have some time to talk with me this morning. It's nothing important or urgent. I mean, it's important to me, not urgent. Does that make sense?"

Margo chuckled. "Sure. Do you want me to come over by you or do you want to come over here to the Governor's Mansion? Jace had to go to work early today."

Carley laughed. "I still can't believe you live in the Governor's Mansion. That is so ridiculous."

Margo laughed. "I know. I can't believe it either. I'm still a little pissed that Jace bought it without hiring a real estate agent and that I missed out on the sale. But I love living here, so I'll forgive him."

Carley laughed. "Well, you just remember if you two ever sell it, I'm the realtor that you call. I get the sale."

"You got it, sis. Why don't you come on over? How long before you can be here?"

"I was just about ready to go to the office now, so how about if I pop over in about 15 minutes?"

"Sounds great. I'll have coffee here for you."

"Thanks. See you in a bit."

Carley hung up the phone, grabbed her purse and laptop, then headed out to her car. That's when she remembered Jace wanted the note and the medallion. She ran back inside to get them. She'd left them on the counter in a bowl.

She grabbed the note and the medallion and ran back out to her car, laying them on the seat. She spotted Hanna's delivery van headed toward the bakery as she neared town and thought cinnamon rolls would go perfectly with her conversation this morning. She followed the van to Hanna's bakery. She hadn't seen Hanna in a while, and she was feeling great this morning. It was a perfect day to reconnect. As she stepped through the door, she received a big smile from Hanna.

"Good mornin! How are you today?" Hanna greeted her.

"I'm great. How are you?"

"We're good. Really good." Hanna smiled and her face lit right up. It was nice to see her friends happy. She wanted that. Happiness...it seemed to evade her in her life, but she was feeling hopeful now.

"That's wonderful. We haven't caught up in a while."

Hanna nodded. "That's so true. Let's rectify that."

"That sounds perfect."

"Okay, what can I help you with?"

Carley smiled. "How about two cinnamon rolls to go, please?"

Hanna laughed. "Sounds good."

Hanna pulled a little box from the back counter, lined it with a wax paper sheet, and deftly set her giant cinnamon rolls inside. As Carley saw the size of them, she silently mused she should have ordered one, and she and Margo could share it. But these were so good, she didn't want to share. Not even with her sister.

Hanna rang up the purchase, and Carley handed her a twenty-dollar bill. As Hanna made change, she said, "How about if I get Grace on the line in a while and plan a Thursday ladies' night out?"

"I think that sounds fantastic. Thanks so much, Hanna."

"Okay. I'll confirm with you later today."

"Thank you. Have a great day!"

"You as well."

She picked up the pretty little box with the most delicious cinnamon rolls ever made and headed to her SUV. She had a girls' night out planned, maybe a new boyfriend, and she was about to eat breakfast at the Governor's Mansion.

She chuckled and shook her head when she thought of that again.

She drove up the road to Margo and Jace's home. The name of the road was Classified Drive. The first time she'd heard that, she thought it was hilarious. Jace had petitioned the city council to have it renamed. Typical Jace.

The driveway was surrounded by trees. There were variations of oak and palm trees as well as smaller shrubs that were interesting to look at, but there was some longer brush underneath. She knew without a doubt she wouldn't go walking through those trees anytime soon. Who knew what lay in there?

She pulled to a stop at the front door, grabbed her box

and her purse, and was surprised to see the door open before she even made it to the top step. Her sister stood there looking gorgeous as ever wearing yellow slacks and a white sleeveless blouse with a gold chain. She looked every bit a governor's wife, even though she wasn't.

"Good morning. You look like you fit right in here." Carley hugged her sister and Margo laughed.

"I do fit here. We've made this our home, and we love it."

"That's good. I'm glad to hear it."

"I brought cinnamon rolls. Hanna says hello, and she would like us to get together on Thursday for a girls' night. Are you up for that?"

"I am. I think we were just talking about that, weren't we?"

"Oh, that's right, we were, but we didn't set any plans, so now we have plans. Pencil it into your calendar."

"All right, sounds good. Let's go out back. I've got the table set and coffee's ready to go. We can sit in the Florida Room and chat."

"Sounds good."

Carley followed her sister to the back of the house. Margo poured them each a cup of coffee and Carley put a cinnamon roll on each of the two plates, then carried them to the Florida room. Margo followed her with the coffee. The room was warm and all windows. It was peaceful and of course, beautifully decorated.

They made themselves comfortable on the sofa. Both put their legs up on the coffee table and looked out the windows at the landscaping. The flowers were in bloom. Birds and butterflies flitted from flower to flower.

Carley really enjoyed sitting back here with her sister and looking out at all they'd done. She and Margo had spent hours back here changing up the landscaping. Margo could have hired someone, and she did for some things, but she wanted her hand in the gardens, and Carley was eager to help her. It was a bonding experience, not that they needed one. They were the closest to each other of all her sisters.

"So, tell me what's on your mind, Carley," Margo said.

Carley took a deep breath and let it out slowly. "When did you know you wanted to have a relationship with Jace?"

Margo turned her head and stared at her. She swallowed the bite of cinnamon roll she had in her mouth and set her plate on the coffee table.

"Um, I don't know that I actually had a decision to make. I didn't have a day that I knew I wanted to have a relationship with him. It just sort of happened, I guess. If you recall I didn't like him much in the beginning."

Carley laughed. "Oh, I recall."

"I don't know. It just, I guess it was meant to be. It was kind of like peeling an onion.. He kept showing me sides of himself that I didn't or hadn't seen before or didn't expect to see. And each time a layer of the onion was peeled back, I liked more and more what I saw. Does that explain anything to you?"

Carley nodded. "Yeah, it does."

"So why are you asking?"

"I don't know." Margo stopped her with her hand up.

"I think you do know. Let me see if I can fill in some blanks." Margo twisted to see her clearly. "You like Mason. He likes you. I could tell the way you acted with each other yesterday. Also, the way you look at each other. Little smiles here and there. Am I getting warm?"

"Yes, you're getting warm. And after everybody left yesterday, we slept together."

Margo sucked in a deep breath and her brows shot up. "Get out of here! Did you really?"

Carley's face heated. It had nothing to do with the weather. And as she looked at her sister, she swallowed a big lump in her throat. "I did. We did. I wanted to. And he did too. But he kind of, I don't know." She took a breath. "We started kissing and then he pulled away and said he was damaged and wasn't worthy of me, and I didn't deserve to have to put up with him. He has nightmares. And then I, I don't know. I guess I kind of talked him into it. Or told him I didn't care. And I don't, Margo. I don't care. I think he's really a good human. And I think you know I haven't been with a good human like ever. So, he appeals to me in so many ways. But I hope I didn't make a mistake."

"A mistake in what, honey?" Margo asked.

Carley turned and put her left leg on the sofa with her left arm on the back, so she could see Margo full on. "I mean he hesitated, and I sort of insisted. I just thought he was being shy. And maybe I pushed him too fast. And I don't want to scare him off. And I suppose now I kind of feel like, I don't know, a little trampy. I mean, we didn't even have a date yet or anything."

"Oh, well, not everybody dates first before they have sex, sweetheart."

"You and Jace did."

"Well, again, not everybody does it the same way, and I didn't like Jace all that much at first. And I can just tell from seeing Mason every day at work that he is a good human. He's a real good human. And he's smart as a tack. And yeah, he's been through a lot and has PTSD. You already know that, because we saw him have an attack. He doesn't have many at work, but he's had a couple."

Carley considered that. "I was actually considering having Grace bring Chiefy over to see how Chiefy reacted to him. She seems to have a keen sense for someone in need. But I don't want to overstep my bounds either."

"I thought about that too. But Jace told me to mind my own business."

Carley laughed. "Yeah. That's sort of how I feel. It's like I should mind my own business. But I want to help him, Margo. I really want to help him and I want to get to know him better. However, I don't want to be pushy and I don't want to move too fast."

"Well, I think you'll move at the pace you're supposed to move at. If he keeps pulling away, you will sense if he's just not into you or if he's just scared. And let's face it, anybody who's had a rough past may be scared to move forward. The unknown can be scarier when you've had a bad time of it or are reliving your ugly past."

"Yeah, I guess. Well, anyway, we're going to see each other tonight after work. So, we'll have more time to spend with each other."

"There, you have a date. And not too far after having sex the first time." Margo laughed.

"Please don't tell anybody about that. I'm keeping you in confidence."

Margo chuckled. "Honey, I wouldn't tell anybody anything about you. Let's just see how it goes, okay?"

"Yeah, I'll see how it goes."

They finished their coffee and as much of their cinnamon rolls as they could manage. Carley left Margo's house feeling as if a burden had been lifted.

Margo rode with her to the Sandbar, since Jace was already there. Margo would either come home with him or walk home later, they lived so close.

Carley entered the Sandbar expecting to see Mason

behind the bar, but she didn't see him. She had to admit she felt a little letdown.

She followed Margo to the office, and there was Jace talking to Mason. Carley's face heated, not expecting to see him there. And now, seeing him again for the first time since yesterday and knowing what she had told Margo. She wasn't quite sure how to greet him.

"Good morning." Mason grinned at her.

"Good morning."

Jace looked between the two of them, kissed Margo, and then said to Mason, "So you let me know if you have any questions. I think if we maneuver that stuff around in the back room the way we discussed, we'll be fine."

"Sounds good. I'll get it taken care of."

"Thanks, Mason."

Mason glanced at both her and Margo, then nodded and left the room.

Margo asked Jace, "What was that all about?"

"Well, Kaysen called in sick today, and I had a lot for him to do, so I called Mason to update him, and he offered to come in early and help unload the delivery truck. The storeroom is a mess, and Mason likes things in their place, so he's actually going to go through and organize it. I can always count on Mason, and I'm grateful for that."

Margo smiled. She turned to Carley quickly and grinned and then sat at her desk.

"Carley brought you the note and the medallion."

Carley shook her head to think about the task at hand and pulled the medallion and note out of her purse. She handed them to Jace and avoided eye contact. She felt embarrassed from the way he looked at her and Mason.

She found the courage to ask, "Can I see the video to see

who it was that put the note on my car to see if I recognize him?"

"Sure."

Mason stepped back in. "Sorry, I didn't mean to eavesdrop, but I'd like to see it too."

"Of course, " Jace responded.

Jace cued up the video and they watched the man as he approached her car from the road. He looked around and then he stuck the note under her windshield wiper. He then put his hands around his eyes and looked in the windows all around the vehicle. The driver's seat, the back seat behind the driver, the back window. He walked around the passenger side back seat and then the passenger seat. Then he turned around and walked back toward the road.

Jace stopped the video and stood to look at her. "I watched more of it to see if he had a car and drove past, so I could give that to the police, but he didn't. I don't know where he walked to. There isn't much down that way. I have a call into Grace because her rentals are down there. I'd like to know who she has renting to this week. I think he was looking in your vehicle to see if you had the medallion lying in there somewhere. I don't know what he would have done if he would have seen it in the car. Maybe try to break your windows to get in. I don't know."

Jace continued. His eyes landed on Mason's then he looked at her. "And it's kind of weird that he didn't sit in the parking lot and wait for you, which I'm glad he didn't. Do you recognize him?"

"I do. That's the guy who was watching me pull out of my office parking lot the other day."

Jace nodded and looked over at Mason.

Mason said, "Yep, that's the guy I saw running from the building."

"You're sure?"

"I'm absolutely sure. Actually, he was wearing the same clothes."

"Alright, well, I'm headed over to the police department with this on a thumb drive and the note, so that they can see what's going on. Maybe they know who he is, but Carley, in the meantime, please make sure you're never alone when you're out and about. I know that's hard with your job, but just be extra vigilant, okay? Keep your phone in your hand with your thumb hanging over the nine in case you have to call 911. If you can bring someone with you for showings or anywhere you go, try and do that, okay?"

She shrugged. "Okay, It's hard to bring someone with me, but I can make sure that I have safety procedures in place. I'll carry my phone close. I always put the name of whoever I'm meeting and the address and phone number in the computer, so Addison always knows where I am. If I don't check in shortly after the showing, she calls me to make sure everything is okay. We do have that system in place."

"Okay, well, that's good. But like I said, if Addison or someone can go with you, that's probably better. I don't mean to scare you, but we don't know what this guy wants, other than possibly this medallion."

Jace looked down at the medallion in his hand, and he turned it around. "I've never seen anything like this."

He handed it to Mason. "Have you ever seen anything like this?"

Mason turned it over in his hand and stared at it. "No. I haven't seen anything like this either. It seems like the embossing is worn down. It's old."

"Yeah, I think so too. But police might have a database

that they can match it in some way. All right, well, I'm going to run this over then. Thank you for bringing it by Carley."

Carley looked somewhat relieved before saying "Actually, thank you for taking care of this. I do appreciate it."

Jace kissed Margo and stepped from the office. Mason followed.

Carley hugged Margo. "I love you, sis. Thank you for everything. I'll see you later."

"Mind what Jace said, Carley. Be safe no matter what."

"I will. I promise."

She walked out, and Mason was standing by the door. "Again, not eavesdropping, but I also wanted to ask you to please be extra cautious, just in case. It seems like all he wants is this medallion, but he doesn't know you don't have it anymore. I don't even know how he knew you did have it."

"I don't either, and it's weird. When I pulled it up, it was in the bedroom closet in your condo, and it was wedged between the carpeting and the wall. It took me a little while to wiggle it out."

"Could he have been there watching you?"

She swallowed. "I propped the door open. He might have been, but if that was the case, why didn't he just ask me for it?"

"I don't know." He sighed. "I don't know, Carley. Maybe when I walked in, I scared him away from whatever it was he had planned."

She blew out a breath. "Ugh, that's terrible. But, okay, I'll be careful, I promise."

"So other than the showing that you have this afternoon at the condo, do you have anything else today?"

"No, today is about paperwork, mostly."

"Okay, is there any way you can make the showing at the condo a little bit later tonight? That way I can be there."

"Well, he said that was the only time he had available. Quinn told me landscapers are going to be there all day until dark, so there'll be plenty of people around. If my showing is creepy, I'll ask one of the landscapers to come in with me."

"Well, that's not perfect, but all right. I'll be home as soon as I can. Please keep your phone in your hand."

"I promise I will. I'll see you later then."

She walked out of the door, feeling a little nervous, but also a little excited that he cared, and a little creeped out.

16

Mason spent his day organizing the storeroom and unloading the truck of supplies that had come in. After moving to his condo yesterday, this seemed like more of the same.

One thing his Army and medical careers taught him: there's a place for everything, and everything should be in its place. He was a firm believer in that.

He stood back after the last box was unpacked and felt proud. He'd done a damned nice job, and the storeroom had never been more organized than it was right this minute. Jace stepped into the storeroom and whistled.

"Wow, would you look at this?"

Mason grinned from ear to ear. "Right?"

"It looks fantastic. I don't recall it ever looking this organized. Thank you."

Mason nodded and soaked up the praise. "Thank you and you're welcome. I'm rather proud of this."

Jace patted him on the back. "You should be. I'm taking a picture. You want in?"

Mason chuckled. "Naw. Go ahead."

Jace snapped some pictures then Mason turned to leave. "I'll go get the bar situated for lunch."

"Thanks, Mason."

"Do you mind me asking what happened at the police station today with the medallion and note?"

Jace turned and stared at him. His face grew warm under his scrutiny. Jace grinned. "Are you two an item?"

Now his ears burned too. "I don't know."

Jace nodded. "Okay."

"It's complicated."

Jace chuckled. "Yeah." He swiped his hands through his hair and huffed out a breath. "It doesn't have to be though."

Mason swallowed. "Right."

Jace nodded. "So, they are looking into it. They didn't know the man in the video, but they'll be watching. I also told them where Carley works and lives. They'll be driving by her place of business and her house regularly to make sure everything looks okay. I've texted her and told her that."

Mason felt a bit of relief, but that might not be enough if the man got inside somehow. He'd felt a bit unsettled today about all of this. What if that man got to her before he or the police could?

Mason closed the storeroom door and headed out to the bar. He still had friends he'd served with in the Army. A couple of them were training soldiers now. They'd still have contacts with security professionals. Maybe he should consider that.

What he knew was he liked being around Carley. She was amazing. And just seeing her this morning and texting with her, made him happy. When was the last time he'd felt happy?

It had been a long damn time, just to be happy over nothing.

Was Jace right? Was he making it too complicated?

The bar was busy during lunch, and he found himself watching the door in case Carley came in. He wanted to see her right away if she did. But, as the time rolled on, she didn't, and a weird sadness filled his gut.

He finished up the lunch shift, restocked the bar, and managed the few customers sitting in the bar day drinking. Jace stepped behind the bar and nodded.

"If you want to knock off early today, go ahead. I can handle the bar and Margo said she could help if we got busy. Since you came in and worked your ass off in the storeroom, go home and relax, or get ready for your date."

Mason's cheeks heated. "How did you..."

Jace laughed. "My wife and your girlfriend are sisters. There are few secrets between them."

He glanced at his watch. Two-thirty. That was about the time Carley had the showing at the condo. Maybe he could be there with her.

He hustled out to his truck and drove out to the barracks. As he pulled into the lot, he saw Carley's SUV in the last spot in the parking lot. He saw there were landscaping trucks in the back lots when he first pulled into the main driveway. There were landscapers milling all around and four of them worked on the front building, which was his building. It was looking wonderful. He was happy once again he'd purchased this place. It seemed that all the good things revolved around his buying this condo. He'd finally met Carley face to face and look how good that turned out so far. Plus, he'd slept last night. Likely, not having to worry about the other tenants propping open a security door and the lack of noise suited him better. It would be better suited to anyone, actually.

He entered the building and could hear Carley's voice. They were at the condo across from his. He quietly walked down the corridor as he listened to her explain the features of the condo. He was proud of her.

The male voice, though, seemed a bit edgy.

"So when they started building these condos, did they have to dig up the ground underneath?"

"No. The barracks were in place. They just gutted the inside then restructured and built the walls as you see them now."

"So, there was no digging involved?"

"No, there was no digging involved."

"All right. And what about for telephone lines and cable lines and whatnot?"

Mason's brows furrowed. What weird questions.

"Well, there aren't telephone lines anymore. Everything is basically wireless. You'll have your phone service provider, and they either have towers or fiber optics in place. I do believe they laid the fiber optics in the beginning here, and the only digging that was done was with a trencher. The ground was overturned, the fiber laid in, and it was covered up in one pass. So, I guess some digging was done, but not in the sense that they brought in heavy equipment."

The man wasn't finished asking questions. "So who did all the building of these barracks?"

"Quinn Kurtz Construction is the builder. Is there something in particular I can help you with? You seem to be searching for some particular information, and I'm happy to help you find that out."

"No, I don't think so. I just wondered."

"Okay. Should we have a look at the common area? I can

explain to you a little bit about what is going to happen out there."

"Sure."

Mason stopped at his door and unlocked it. The man walked out first, and then Carley exited. She had the door propped open. He was proud of her for that. She unpropped it, put the stopper in her purse, and grinned when she saw him. They stared at each other for a long time. He wanted to kiss her. Hold her close.

Instead, he smiled at her and said, "Nice job."

She smiled and whispered, "Thank you." She followed her customer down the hallway. The man turned and stared down the hallway, and Mason's stomach twisted.

He looked familiar, and he didn't look friendly. Mason relocked his door and followed Carley down the hall.

She explained about the common area, what they were going to be doing with the glass walls, and how it would be private and available to rent for special occasions. She asked him if he had questions.

"No."

"No questions?"

"I want to think on it, okay? I also want to see what the landscapers are doing outside."

"Okay. I can go out with you. You have my information and can get in touch with me anytime."

"All right, yeah."

He turned and walked out the main door, and Carley followed him out, but not without a glance Mason's way.

Mason followed behind Carley. He hung back, but he wanted to be close. Where did he know this guy from?

The man stopped and watched the landscapers in front drop a couple of plants into holes they'd dug. "Well, what are they doing?"

She cocked her head to the side and responded to the ridiculous question. It was clear to see what they were doing.

But, ever the professional, Carley smiled. "They are putting in the landscaping. Not all these condos are finished yet, but because we have residents living here now, Quinn wanted it to look nice for our current residents. So, we're working on the landscaping. The security system is partially installed and will be completed tomorrow. The upstairs condos will be finished within the next three or four weeks."

"Alright."

He slowly walked around the edge of the newly planted landscaping, and Carley followed him. Mason followed her. He had a weird feeling in the pit of his stomach about this guy. And that nagging feeling he'd seen him somewhere before.

One of the landscapers stopped digging. He knelt down, holding the base of the plant in place, as his hands swiped dirt into the hole. A shiny object glistened in the dirt and Carley bent down and picked it up. She looked at it, turning it over in her hand. Her brows furrowed.

Her customer said, "What's that?"

She responded, "I don't know. Looks like a thumb drive or something. I'll give it to Quinn."

"Well, I'd like to see it."

"Um, it's just a thumb drive. And it belongs to the owner of the condos, and that's Quinn Kurtz, so I'll give it to him."

Not to be dismissed, the man asked again, "I'd like to see it, please."

Mason stepped forward and placed himself between Carley and this man. He looked at him, noting his military haircut and straight posture. His blue eyes were unfriendly and they were cold.

He said, "She'll give it to Quinn. I don't know why that bothers you."

"It doesn't bother me. I just wanted to see it."

Mason decided this conversation was finished. "And she showed it to you, and that's all there is to it."

"Right. Well, I'll be in touch, Ms. Page."

"Okay. Sounds good. Thank you for coming this afternoon. And certainly, if you have any questions, let me know."

"Yes, I said I'll be in touch."

He stalked off to his car, and Mason watched him the entire way. Tightness in his chest and a pit in his stomach told him this man was not friendly. As he pulled away, Mason quickly memorized his license plate number, then glanced down at Carley.

He asked softly, "Should we go inside?"

"Sure."

He placed his hand at the small of her back, and they strode inside together. He unlocked his door, and they stepped into his condo.

Mason locked the door again, then looked out the living room window to see if the man had come back.

Glancing around the parking area that he could see from his window, he was satisfied the man wasn't lurking out there. He walked over to the counter, pulled a sheet of paper and pen from the top drawer and scribbled the license plate number as well as the make and model of the vehicle.

Carley walked over. "What are you doing?"

"I wrote down his license plate number and the make and model of the vehicle."

"Why?"

"Something's not right with him. Do you mind if I take a look at the thumb drive you found?"

"Oh, no."

She held her hand out. It was a little dirty. She strolled over to the sink to wash her hands, and he took a napkin and brushed off the thumb drive.

It was heavy-duty, scratched up, and had a bit of weight to it.

"Carley, this is a military thumb drive."

"Military? How do you know?"

"Well, I have some security clearances, and they use this type of thumb drive. They're specially encrypted. You'd have to know the protocols and the software to be able to get into it. It shouldn't have been laying in the ground."

"Right. Was there anything else there?"

"No, I didn't see anything else. I just saw this glint when the landscaper was brushing the dirt away into the hole."

"Hang tight. I'm going to go ask the landscaper."

Mason strode out of his condo and the building. The same landscaper was still there. He stopped near the younger man. "Did you find anything else near this building or around this hole that would have been lying near where this thumb drive was found?"

The landscaper was maybe in his very early twenties. He nodded his head. "Yeah, we found this old box here, too."

He bent over to a pile of brush and roots they'd been pulling up and pulled a dirty green cardboard box from the top of the pile, not much bigger than the thumb drive. It was broken and slashed.

"I'm sorry," the young man said. "I think my shovel damaged it a little bit. That's probably how the thumb drive fell out of it. Is it yours?"

"Not mine, but I know who it might belong to, and I'll give him the box, too. Thanks."

"Sure."

"And there wasn't anything else found in or around here?"

"No, no, there was nothing else."

"Okay, thank you. I appreciate it. Everything is looking good."

"Thanks."

Mason swallowed the lump in his throat as he walked back down the hallway to where Carley was. She stood in the kitchen watching the door, and when he walked in, her eyebrows rose into her bangs.

"Was there something else?"

"Yeah, this box." He held up the small, ripped box. "The landscaper says his shovel hit it and cut through it. This thumb drive was probably inside, and it fell out when they were shifting the dirt back and forth."

"Well, who do you think it belongs to?" Her eyes were seriously distracting.

"Well, I'm not real sure why it would be here, Anyone who would have stayed in these barracks back in the day would not have had the type of security clearance that would have allowed them access to something like this. In my gut, something tells me *"There's something rotten in Denmark."* I'm going to take it to Jace and Quinn. If they don't have the correct contacts, I still have some security clearances and friends inside I can get this to. They might be able to tell me where it came from or where it belongs."

"Okay."

He looked at Carley and grinned. "You seem to have a penchant for finding things that don't belong to you."

She grinned. "Well, it seems so. It's never been my forte

before, but then again, I found you. Do you belong to someone else?"

They looked into each other's eyes for a long time. He liked looking into her eyes. Maybe it was his new favorite thing to do.

He didn't respond though. All he did was shake his head.

17

She stepped closer to Mason. They stood toe to toe for a few minutes, then he bent down and kissed her lips. She liked it. She moved into the circle of his arms, and he froze.

"Hang tight. I need to take a shower. I've been working my ass off at the Sandbar and I'm dirty."

She grinned. "I can wash your back."

His beautiful brown eyes changed. They deepened in color, and he swallowed. Her stomach twirled as she waited for him to say something. She was seriously forward with him, but she wanted him. She wanted to do all things with him.

When he responded, his voice cracked. "Okay."

She smiled and began unbuttoning her blue blouse. He watched her intently as she slowly shrugged her blouse down her arms. She hung her bouse on the dining room chair, then began unfastening the button and zipper on her slacks. His eyes dipped down to watch her fingers, and his nostrils flared when she let her silky slacks fall down her hips. She slowly bent to pick up her slacks, folded them, and dropped them over the dining room chair as well. When she turned back to Mason, he stood transfixed, staring at her body.

"You're sexy, Carley Page."

She smiled. It felt good that he enjoyed watching her. "I think you're sexy too, Mason Thompson."

She slid her hands behind her and unfastened her bra strap. His eyes waited on her breasts for the showing. She let her bra slide down her arms, catching it before it fell to the ground. She lay that over her slacks on the chair.

Mason's hand reached out and touched her breasts. He cupped each one in a hand and gently squeezed. His thumbs played over her nipples, and she closed her eyes, enjoying the feel. Her eyes flew open when she felt his warm wet mouth suck one of her breasts into his mouth. Her hands dug into his hair as his mouth plundered her breasts. He moved his mouth from one to the other, sucking in deeply as he did. It went straight to her core. The feeling of his mouth on her body was incredible.

He pulled away and she groaned.

He chuckled. "Finish."

Her eyes locked with his. He didn't say anything, he didn't smile, he waited. It was sexy.

She tucked her thumbs into her panties and slid them down her legs. She balanced on one foot and removed them from the other leg, then repeated. She lay her panties over her bra.

She turned to see him eagerly staring at her body. She'd never been shy about her body; she knew she looked good. Even though she'd gained a few pounds over the years, she still looked good.

He undid his jeans and pulled them down, tugging his underwear with them. Then he quickly stepped forward, scooped her into his arms, and lifted her to his waist. She wrapped her legs around his waist and instantly felt him position his cock at her entrance.

She kissed his lips; he kissed her back. He pulled her body down onto his cock slowly. She held him tightly around his shoulders. The position was awkward but sexy as hell.

His hands gripped her ass and moved her up and down, though he couldn't pull out as far as he had last night. But it felt incredible. Her breathing came in spurts as her orgasm drew close. Then he lifted her off him and set her on the floor. It took her a few moments to realize what happened, and she started to protest. He spun her around, and she gripped the counter. With his feet, he slid her feet further apart.

"Stick your ass out for me, Carley."

She did as he asked, about to protest that she didn't want to do that without lubricant. But he didn't slide into her ass, he slid into her pussy nice and slow. The firmness of his cock and the thickness spread her perfectly. She moaned as he moved in and out of her. Then, his fingers wrapped around her body and pressed into her clit. That was just about it.

He found that perfect spot and rhythmically circled it as his cock slid in and out.

Her orgasm rolled over her quickly and she gasped as she came. He didn't stop, he kept going. His fingers worked her faster and her clit was so sensitive she gasped as he added pressure.

He whispered in her ear. "Do it again, Carley."

She could smell them. Their scent together was incredible. She'd never walk into this kitchen again without thinking about this right here.

She cried out her orgasm as he slid into her again and held himself inside. He moaned and jerked a few times as he came inside of her. His breathing ragged near her ear.

She dropped her head into her hands on the cool granite countertop. She closed her eyes, waiting for her breathing to return to normal. But before that happened, Mason spun her around, picked her up, and carried her to the bathroom. He set her on the floor, reached in, turned the water on, and then stared at her.

"You are so fucking sexy."

She swallowed to moisten her throat. "So are you."

He grinned and she loved that little grin of his. As soon as steam rolled out of the shower, he took her hand and pulled her gently into the shower. "You said you'd wash my back."

She chuckled. "I'd like my back washed too."

He growled out. "I'll wash your entire body."

Perfect.

***

Carley's phone rang and she tapped the button on her steering wheel to answer it.

"Hello, Carley Page, how can I help you?"

"Hello, Carley this is Layton Terry, I was with you yesterday. You were showing me condo number five. I'd like to take another look at it this evening, please."

"Okay." Her heart dropped. She didn't really care to show him the condo alone. Yesterday was weird. "I have an appointment at five, but PJ could be at the condo at six o'clock, would that work for you?"

"Actually I'd like it a little bit later, I have to work myself and can't get there until about eight o'clock."

"Oh, it's almost dark by eight o'clock. I've been barred from showing the condos after dark due to the current owners and their privacy. Are you sure we can't be there a little sooner?"

"No, that's the soonest I can get there."

"Well, maybe I can answer some questions for you. What is it that you need to see?"

He hesitated a moment and her stomach did somersaults.

"I actually would just like to see the place again and then go ahead and put in an offer, but I want to refresh myself with the size of the closets and the fixture finishings before I make a final decision."

Carley swallowed. She didn't like him, and she got a weird feeling from him. Maybe Margo could take a break and come with her. Mason would be working till eight or nine. Maybe he could get off at eight.

"Well, let me see if I can find someone to come with me, then I can give you a call back."

He hesitated for a moment. "Why do you need someone to come with you?"

"Well, it's just after dark, a girl can never be too careful, you know?"

"Hmm, all right. Well, I'll wait to hear from you."

The phone call ended, and she tapped the button on her steering wheel to end the call. She rotated her head on her shoulders. He just gave off a weird vibe, but like Margo said yesterday, people who have had a bad past may be reluctant to offer friendship or be congenial. He certainly wasn't trying hard to be congenial, that was a fact.

She parked her car at the back of her office building. She glanced all around to make sure no one was hanging around, and as soon as she felt sure no one was around, she strode in the back door.

Addison was sitting at her desk with a smile on her face.

"Hi, Carley. Police Chief Trey Fielding called you a while ago. He'd like you to give him a call right away, please."

Carley nodded. "Okay, thanks."

Addison cocked her head. "Is everything okay?"

Carley stopped progress to her office and turned. She moved to stand before Addison. She swallowed a lump in her throat and shrugged. "So, I found a scratched-up old medallion between the carpeting and the wall at the condo that Mason just bought. Some guy left a note on my windshield saying I had something that belonged to him. I then saw him watching me pull out of my parking spot in back yesterday. I told Jace about it and he asked for the note and medallion. He looked at his security cameras and found the man putting the note on my windshield at the Sandbar. He took it to Chief Fielding yesterday, so that's probably what the chief wants to talk to me about."

"Well, that's creepy. If he was standing out back, how about we make sure the back door is locked at all times?" she asked.

"I'm totally fine with that. I'll go check it right now." Carley went to the back door and made sure it was locked. She came back to Addison's desk.

Addison said "Layton Terry just called and was looking for you. I gave him your cell phone number. He said it was important that he speak with you."

Just the mention of his name made a knot form in Carley's throat. "Yes, he called me. He wants to see the condo again tonight but not until eight o'clock. I don't really care to meet him that late."

"I don't blame you, he's weird."

"Well, he certainly is different, I'll say that, and he's not very friendly. Yesterday I found what looks like a thumb drive in the dirt the landscapers were digging up around the building. He became increasingly weird about seeing it. I told him I would give it to Quinn. It certainly wasn't his, and it wasn't mine, but he kept insisting he see it. I'm grateful Mason was there. He stepped between us and told the man it wasn't anything for him to worry about."

Addison kind of shivered "Well, that's creepy too. Maybe we should lock the front door also."

Carley laughed. "How will customers come in?"

"Well, it's not like we have a drove of walk-in customers. I'm right here. I can unlock the door for anyone who comes up."

Carley nodded "You know that's not a bad idea, why don't you go ahead and do that. I'm gonna go check my voicemail and emails and call Chief Fielding."

18

Mason felt his phone buzz in his pocket and pulled it out to see who texted. He grinned when he saw Carley's name. He'd been thinking about her nonstop today. They'd had a hot night last night. Sex. Shower. They ordered food to be delivered and watched a movie. Afterwards, they had sex again, and she slept over. He basically told her she had to stay over since he didn't want her out there alone in her house at night. Initially, he'd worried about his nightmares, but she told him if it was bad, she'd sleep on the couch. He relaxed after that. He only had one nightmare, and it wasn't a bad one.

This morning, she woke him up, sitting on top of him. His cock roared to life, and the instant she felt it, she slid herself on him. Best way to wake up...ever.

He read her text.

"Hey, Layton Terry wants to see the condo at eight tonight. He insisted on that time. Do you think you'll be off to join me?"

"I'll make sure. Don't go in without me there."

"Okay. See you later."

"Looking forward to it."

She sent a smiling face and replied.

"I've been thinking about you all day."

His heart swelled and his mind went back to this morning. And suddenly he couldn't wait to see her again. Actually, it wasn't sudden at all. He tapped out,

"I've been thinking about you too."

She sent another smiley face. He waited in case she was going to send something more. She didn't so he pocketed his phone and continued working.

He called a cleaning company to go into his old apartment and clean it up. Then he called his now former landlord and told him a cleaning company was coming in tomorrow and he should try to rent out his apartment. He was obligated to a sixty-day notice and he acknowledged that. He'd pay the two months' rent if he had to, but he also knew it would rent quickly. He'd likely not have to pay anything at all, so would let the chips fall where they may.

Jace stepped behind the bar. "Good morning."

Mason grinned. "Morning. Do you have a minute?"

"Sure. We have time before we open, let's head back to the office."

He followed Jace to the office, pulling the thumb drive

out of his pocket that Carley had found. As they stepped into the office, Margo was sitting at her desk on her computer. She turned and smiled. "Morning."

"Good morning." He nodded.

Jace turned to him, "Is it okay if Margo stays or does this need to be private?"

He shook his head, "It's not private, and it's her office, too, so I'd feel bad asking her to leave." He held his hand out to Jace. "Carley found this on the grounds of the condos last night. It's military-grade. I recognize it, and whoever had it originally, had some security clearance. And when that place was a barracks, no one with that type of clearance would have stayed there."

Jace turned it over in his hand, then pulled the cap off of it. "Did you look at it?"

"No."

He pushed it into the side of his computer and a Military Intelligence logo appeared on the screen. Jace turned his head and stared at Mason. "Holy shit."

"Right."

Jace clicked on the logo, and a sign-in window appeared. He stood and huffed out a deep breath. "I don't have contacts with super-high clearance anymore. Do you?"

"I have a couple of people I can contact."

"Okay. Who else knows about this thumb drive?"

"The landscaper who was there and a client of Carley's named Layton Terry. That guy Terry seemed weird about it. He kept asking to see it sand what she was going to do with it. It creeped both of us out."

"Okay. Tell you what, I'll put this in the safe. You call your contacts and see who we can get this to."

Mason nodded. "Thanks. I feel better knowing it's hidden and secure until we can hand it over."

Mason stepped out of the office and pulled his phone from his pocket. He dialed up his former Army Lieutenant, Ethan Dougherty. Putting his phone to his ear, he stepped into the storeroom where it was private.

"Hello, Mason Thompson. How are you doing?"

"Hello, Lieutenant. I'm fine."

Ethan's laugh sounded so good to hear over the phone. He'd always been a happy guy. "I'm not your Lieutenant anymore."

Mason grinned. "I'm aware. It's a sign of respect you know."

"Thank you. It's good to hear from you. What's going on?"

"I found, or I should say, my girl..." He swallowed. "My girlfriend found a military thumb drive. My boss put it in his computer and the Department of Military Intelligence logo came up on the screen. I don't know what's on the thumb drive, but it was buried in the dirt around an old barracks here in town that has been turned into condos. I live there. The barracks was decommissioned about twelve years ago."

"Interesting. Where are you?"

"In Blossom Springs, Florida."

"Okay. Let me do some checking on my end. I'll get back to you by the end of the day with a plan. Can you keep it safe?"

"Yes. I work at a bar called the Sandbar, and my boss has it in the safe."

"You work in a bar?"

Mason immediately began sweating. He'd forgotten for a moment about his situation. He froze, not sure what to say. Ethan spoke again. "I think we have some catching up to do."

"Yes, sir."

"Hmm." There was a brief silence, and then Ethan spoke again. "I'll be in touch with you later today, Mason. Thank you for calling me."

"Of course. Thank you."

"Nice talking with you."

"Yes sir...Ethan. It was nice talking with you."

The call ended, and Mason pressed his back against the wall and closed his eyes. What did it mean that he'd forgotten to explain before he told Ethan about the thumb drive? Of course, Ethan knew Mason had left the Army. But the last he'd seen Ethan, at their annual get-together three years ago, he was still a surgeon. He'd stopped going to the annual gatherings, embarrassed about his PTSD and then his leaving his job at Presbyterian Hospital in Maryland.

He dragged a deep breath into his lungs, pushed himself off the wall, and strode out to the bar to finish set-up for the day.

The door to the Sandbar opened and a man and woman hurried in and shut the door. They seemed upset. Mason moved out from behind the bar and made his way over to them. They stood by the door watching it.

"Can I help you with something?"

The man turned to him. He swallowed and nodded. "There's some guy out there walking in between the cars. As we walked toward the building he followed us. My wife..." he glanced at the woman next to him. "was scared."

"What's he wearing?"

Mason turned the handle on the door before the man was finished. He hustled out to the parking area and saw the back of the man's head hurrying away from the Sandbar. He recognized him. The same hair and still wearing the same clothes.

Pulling his phone from his pocket, he dialed the Blossom Springs Police Department.

"Blossom Springs PD. How can I help you?"

"This is Mason Thompson. I work at the Sandbar. The man you're looking for who put a note on Carley Page's car is here now."

"I'll send an officer over right away."

"Thank you."

He hung up and followed the man, keeping a distance from him in case he was armed. The man turned and saw him, then took off running. He had a bit of a limp to him, as if he had a bad leg or had hurt himself. Mason took off after him, grateful he jogged a couple of times a week. He gained on the man, then, as if he'd done this before, he ducked into a small patch of tall brush that led up to Sid and Grace's place.

He didn't have Sid's phone number, nor Grace's but he knew Jace did. He stopped in front of the patch of brush and called Jace as he watched for movement.

"Hey, Mason, what's up? Some customers said you were following someone."

"Yeah. The man who put the note on Carley's windshield had scared a couple of customers. I've called the police, and they're on their way, but he dove into some tall brush that leads up to Sid and Grace's house. I don't know if they're home to warn them. I don't have their numbers."

"I'll call. I hear sirens now, stay where you are, and I'll send them up the road."

The call ended, and he craned his neck to see if he could spot something moving. The adrenaline raced through his bloodstream, and he felt the flush of heat envelope his body. Of course, it was plenty hot outside, but this was internal.

The sirens grew louder, but he didn't take his eyes off the brush.

A police cruiser stopped on the road and the officer neared him slowly.

"I'm Officer Isak Voss. Can I help you?"

Mason was afraid to turn away from the area in case he missed something. He also didn't want to be rude. Finally, he reached forward and held his hand out to shake the officer's hand. "I'm Mason Thompson. I called. He ran in there."

Officer Voss stared at the area and heaved out a deep sigh. "I hate this."

"I'm aware. I'm also not terribly familiar with this area other than I know Sid and Grace Hoffman live up there. This piece of land..." He pointed to the brushy area. "Meanders along the cliff and separates their place from the water below."

Officer Voss nodded. "Yep. That's correct. Also, much further in there, the terrain gets very steep. So, now we have to decide whether to go up or down."

Mason nodded. "If it helps, I called Jace to tell Sid this guy is around, so up is likely covered."

Officer Voss grinned. "That helps." He strode toward the bottom edge of the brush, and Mason stood watch, not sure what he should do to help other than stand there in case the man came back out.

After a few minutes, he heard Officer Voss yell, "Stop and put your hands in the air. I said, stop! Stop. Stop. Stop."

Then a gunshot rang out and Mason's legs crumbled beneath him.

19

Carley's phone rang, and she saw Margo's name on her screen. Tapping to answer the call, she cheerfully said, "Hey, sis. What's up?"

Margo's voice was a bit stressed. "Carley, honey, don't be alarmed but Mason had a PTSD attack. He chased the man who put the note on your car and the man ran. Officers went in search of him and shot at him. It triggered an attack for Mason. He fell in the road."

"Oh my God. Is he okay? Where is he now? I have to get to him. Where is he?"

"Listen, Carley. Listen to me. You can't run in here panicked. You need to be calm and supportive. Do you understand?"

She closed her eyes. Panic was the first thing she had done. What would happen if she panicked in front of him when he had an attack? Would it make it worse? Would it make him think she didn't want to be with him? He tried warning her away.

She took a deep breath. "I understand."

"Okay. He's here in the office. Come in the back door, I'll wait for you there."

"Okay."

She didn't say goodbye, she simply rushed from her office and called out to Addison, "I'll be back in a bit."

"Okay."

She hustled out the back door and nearly ran to her SUV. Then she remembered safety and to be calm. She sucked in a deep breath and let it out slowly. She hurried back to the office door and checked to make sure the lock had engaged. Satisfied that it had, she returned to her SUV and climbed into the driver's seat.

She purposely drove slowly to give herself time to calm down. She talked to herself the entire drive, which wasn't that far, only a few blocks. "Be calm. He's not hurt, he had a panic attack. He gets these. It's fine."

Pulling into the parking lot of the Sandbar, she parked closest to the side door near the storeroom. Inside was a hallway that led to either the office or the storeroom. If the bar was full, Jace and Margo could slip in the back way. Also, that's where they unloaded trucks, so everything went to the storeroom rather than the kitchen.

She tried opening the door, but it was locked. She knocked on it in case Margo was waiting for her.

The door opened and her sister's pretty head popped out.

"Hi. Come on in. And remember...calm."

"Is he alright?"

Margo stopped and stared at her for a moment. "Yes. He's fine. He's embarrassed. And he hit his head pretty hard. He's going to have a headache for a day or two."

"Oh. Poor man."

"Right."

Margo turned and continued walking toward the office. She put her hand on the knob and looked at Carley before pushing the door open.

Carley nodded and whispered. "I'm good. Calm. I'm calm."

Margo nodded and pushed the door open.

Mason sat in a chair at the back of the office. He had a bandage on his upper thigh and one on the side of his head. Jace sat in a chair next to him but turned it to face Mason and spoke to him softly. She couldn't hear what Jace was saying. Margo quietly moved to her desk and sat in the chair. Carley swallowed the knot in her throat and eased forward.

She took in the bandages, but she didn't understand them. Mason's eyes opened, and the instant he focused on her, she saw his breathing increase. Deep huffs of breath pushed from his lungs, and she wasn't sure if she should approach him or not. Slowly, his hand rose from where it rested on his thigh, and he held it out to her.

She stepped forward slowly and took his hand in hers. There wasn't a place to sit so she knelt in front of him. "Are you alright?"

"Yeah."

She looked at the bandage on his head, then into his eyes. "Stitches?"

"No."

Nodding, she looked at the bandage on his thigh. "Stitches?"

"Yep."

Her brows rose into her hairline. "Why?"

"Bullet wound."

"You were shot!" Her voice rose.

"Yeah."

Carley turned to stare at Margo. "You didn't tell me that."

"I wanted you to stay calm."

"Calm!"

Margo's brows rose into her bangs and Carley swallowed. She turned back to Mason and looked into his eyes. "What happened?"

"I chased the man who put the note on your car. He dove into some thick brush that leads up to Sid and Grace's house. I called Jace to let them know, then I called the police. Officer Voss went to the bottom of the brush to find him. I waited on the road and heard Voss yell for him to stop and put his hands up. The office yelled again for him to stop, then I heard a gunshot. I fell to the ground. I thought I was having a panic attack, then I felt the pain in my thigh. Officer Voss came out of the brush and saw me lying on the road. It turns out the bullet he fired ricocheted off a rock and hit me. By the time it hit the rock and veered, it was already slowing down, so it's not too bad. The bullet was in my leg but near the surface, so an EMT pulled it out and bandaged me up."

"Why aren't you in the hospital?"

Mason's brows shot into his hair. "For this?" He shrugged. "It's nearly a superficial wound."

"A bullet went into your leg."

"Not all the way."

"Mason..."

He slowly shook his head. "It's honestly not bad, Carley. It'll be sore for a few days. I'll keep it clean and bandaged. I'll be fine."

She took a deep slow breath. "What about your PTSD attack?"

His brows bunched together. "I didn't have one."

"But Margo..." She turned to see her sister staring at her.

"Calm. I wanted you to be calm."

She let out a breath, and her shoulders slumped forward. Mason's fingers lifted her chin, so their eyes met. "It's all good, Carley. I'm going home for the day – boss's orders." He grinned at Jace. "We didn't want you to panic, but I did want to see you."

She smiled softly. "Okay." She stood and brushed her slacks off. "Well, I'm happy your injuries weren't worse. I'm also sorry it happened. Did they find him?"

"No."

Jace chuckled. "But Sid's up there watching."

"Okay."

She looked at Mason once more. "Come on, I'll get you home."

"You'll have to drive me. They gave me pain meds."

She chuckled. "No problem. I can drive you."

Jace grinned while saying "I'll bring his truck by later. Margo can follow and get me home."

"Thank you."

She stood back as Mason stood. He halted and waited to get his equilibrium. Then she stepped up to him and he put his arm around her shoulders. He was only slightly wobbly, and moved slowly, favoring his injured leg. She liked helping him. She liked that he wanted her to help him too.

She leaned forward and opened the door to the outside before stepping back to help him walk through. They limped along at a steady pace to her SUV, where she opened the passenger door and stood nearby, in case he needed assistance getting inside. She closed the door and hustled around the vehicle to get him home.

After climbing inside, she backed from her spot and turned her vehicle toward the Barracks. Mason rested his head on the headrest as she drove. Luckily, he lived close.

"We'll get you inside, then I'll make you something to eat."

"He rolled his head so he could see her. "Oh." He took a deep breath. "I haven't gone grocery shopping yet."

She grinned. "I can take you to my place. I have groceries."

"Okay."

She chuckled. He was being very agreeable. Not that he wasn't usually, but he'd normally say he didn't want to put her out or some other nonsense.

She passed Main Street and headed out of town to her place with a grin on her face.

20

Mason took a deep breath and let it out slowly. He hated this feeling of being a bit out of it. He was also hungry, as he'd missed lunch today.

Carley pulled into her garage and closed the door with the controller on her visor. She glanced at him briefly then smiled. "Hang tight."

He chuckled and watched her hurry around the front of her vehicle and open his door. He heaved himself forward from the passenger seat and set his good leg on the ground. Easing his left leg from the vehicle, he was pleased it didn't hurt that bad. He was fortunate. That bullet could have hit him in the head or the eye or other soft tissue. His leg wasn't that big of a deal.

After standing a moment to gather his stability, he put his arm around Carley's shoulders, and she led him to the door. This was the best part of being injured. Walking with his arm around her shoulders, smelling the fragrance of her hair. The feel of her body pressed tightly to his was nice, too.

She leaned forward and pushed open the door. "Okay, only two steps."

He nodded. Using his non-injured leg first, he stepped up. Then he rested his left leg on the step. He repeated that one more time, and they were inside.

She had a beautiful home. He was surprised at how elegant it was. She walked him to a stool at the counter and helped him ease onto it.

"Would you like something to drink while I make something to eat?"

"Sure. Water is good. My mouth is kind of dry."

She chuckled. "It's the pain killer."

"Yeah."

"So why didn't you go to the hospital?"

"I didn't need to go."

She turned and looked into his eyes. She stared at him for a minute then nodded. She didn't say anything. That would likely come later. He could tell she wanted to say something.

Truth be told, and only to himself, the thought of going into the hospital made his head spin. He hadn't been inside a hospital since he left his job. He wasn't ready to enter a hospital. He still had nightmares about the smell and the sounds of the machines. He just couldn't go in. He knew enough to keep his wound clean and make sure he did what it took to heal.

He watched Carley pull food from the refrigerator and set it on the counter. She pulled a glass from the cupboard and filled it with water from the door in the refrigerator.

Turning she set the glass in front of him and smiled.

"I didn't expect you to live in such a large home."

She laughed. "Neither did I." She shook her head. "Things worked out that way. This was Margo's house.

When she and Logan were married, they built this house and lived here. When he died, and things came out of the woodwork about his affair, this house lost its luster for her. When she and Jace got serious, and she moved in with him, I stayed here. Then, when she and Jace married, she made me an offer I couldn't refuse to purchase the house. I took it. I was in the middle of leaving my deadbeat boyfriend, and the move to a new town seemed the best fit. Plus, I'd be close to my sister."

He nodded as he listened to her story. She smiled often and looked at him a lot. She worked on their dinner, with what seemed little effort.

"Why did you move here?" she asked.

He took a deep breath. "I'd left my job and was looking for a new place to land. My brother had been down here years ago and spoke fondly of it. So, I thought, why not? I love the weather, and I found a great job, though I'm overqualified. However, it suits me. Mixing drinks and chatting is what my wounded soul needed. The change has helped quite a bit. My PTSD attacks are fewer here."

She stopped across the counter from him and smiled brightly. "This place is healing. I'm happy for you and me too. I'm happy for both of us."

He chuckled. "Me too."

He yawned. She cocked her head to the side. "Would you like to lay down while supper is cooking?"

"No. It's..." He looked into her eyes and her smiling face. "Do you mind?"

"Of course not. Come on, I'll get you to the bedroom."

"I'm very sorry I'm not in better shape when you say things like that."

She laughed out loud. "There will be other times, I promise."

He chuckled as he stood, and he put his arm around her as she led him down the hall. They passed by other doors with beds in them, a nice bathroom, and finally, at the end of the hallway was her bedroom.

They stepped through the door, and he glanced around the large room. It was decorated smartly with clean design details. Not that he knew much about decorating. He noticed there weren't a bunch of things on the walls like he'd seen in other homes. They stopped next to the bed, and she eased him down to a sitting position. Kneeling before him, she untied his tennis shoes and set them along the wall. "Do you want to get under the covers?"

He shook his head. "No. I don't want to sleep too long."

"I'll come and get you for supper in about a half hour."

She pulled a blanket from the closet and placed it over him as he laid back. She kissed his lips lightly. Then he closed his eyes and was out.

21

Carley finished prepping the casserole and slid it into the oven. She cleaned up her mess then set the table. She pulled her laptop from its case and opened it on the kitchen counter. She answered a couple of emails then looked at her calendar. She had to show Layton Terry the condo in three hours. She had enough time.

She received a signed offer on one of her listings from another real estate agent in the area and grinned when she saw the offer was the same as the asking price. She forwarded it to her seller with a note, *"We've received a signed offer on your house. Congratulations! Time to pack."*

The oven timer was about to go off, so she opened the oven and pulled the casserole out. She padded down the hall to the bedroom. Standing in the doorway, she watched Mason sleep. His face was relaxed and his breathing was even and strong. He was a handsome one. Incredibly handsome. She allowed herself a couple of minutes to stare at him, then softly stepped next to the bed. She ran her hand down his arm as she softly said, "Hey, there. It's time to get up."

He didn't wake so she spoke a bit louder. "Hey, Mason. Honey, it's time to get up."

He didn't wake but he did move his legs. Then his legs began thrashing, and she stepped back, worrying he'd reinjure his leg, but afraid to get too close. He was having another nightmare. His arms began pushing away from him as if he was pushing something or someone back. His legs kicked almost like he was running. Then he bolted upright and stared across the room for a moment.

Carley swallowed and stepped in his line of vision. "Hey."

He took a deep breath. "Hey."

He scraped his hands through his hair, then down his face. Turning his face toward her he asked, "Did I scare you?"

"No."

His lips frowned for a moment. He twisted and set his feet on the floor with a slight wince. Carley softly announced "supper's ready when you are. The primary bathroom is right down this little hallway to your right. Take your time, it can sit a few minutes."

She turned to leave the room, but he halted her. "Hey."

She turned to him. "Yes."

He grinned. "You were scared."

"I wasn't."

He cocked his head and waited.

"I wasn't. I'm never sure what I should do. Get out of the way. Get in the way. Call out to you." She shrugged. "I don't know what you're pushing away, and I don't want to be replaced as that thing or person."

He let out a deep breath. "Yeah." He looked at his feet then his eyes slid up to hers. "I keep having nightmares about the people I've killed."

"Killed?"

He shrugged. "They were on my operating table, and I couldn't save them. I killed them."

"No, you didn't. That's not killing someone, Mason. You may not have been able to save them, but you didn't kill them."

"In my nightmares, I did, and they're trying to get to me to kill me too."

Her shoulders dropped and she stepped in front of him and knelt. Tipping her head up to look into his beautiful, sad eyes, she smiled softly. "You're not a murderer."

"I didn't help them. That's what I was trained to do. But I didn't do it."

She ran her hands up and down his firm solid arms. "Mason." Taking a deep breath she said, "You were trained to help people who can be helped. Not everyone who comes into your OR is savable. Especially not in a time of war. You were working under hard conditions. Even outside of the war arena, there will be those you just cannot save, no matter how much training you have. When it's our time to go, God will call us home."

His eyes stared into hers for a long time. His watered slightly and he blinked rapidly to dry them. He nodded and swallowed. She raised herself up and touched her lips lightly to his. His hands bracketed her head and his lips moved slightly against hers. It was a sweet kiss. Nice. He rested his forehead against hers.

She wrapped her arms around his waist, and they stayed in that position for some time. Comforting each other. Sharing a moment. A quiet moment that didn't feel awkward. It was sweet. He was such a contrast of emotions. When they had sex, he could take charge. He knew what he wanted and was learning what she wanted. Then, there were times like this when he was completely vulnerable. She liked both Masons.

He pulled back slightly and chuckled. "I'm sorry to break this moment because it's one of the best moments of my life. Comforting and comfortable. But I have to piss."

She chuckled. "Mother Nature calls."

She stood up, then backed away, and he stood and waited to make sure his balance was intact. Then he limped to the ensuite bathroom, and she went out to the kitchen to get supper on the table.

Pulling the salad from the refrigerator, she carried it to the table, then turned to get the dressing from the fridge when Mason appeared in the doorway.

She smiled. "Hey. Take a seat at the table. What can I get you to drink?"

"A beer."

She halted. "Can you have one?"

His brows pinched together. "Because of the pain pills? They were just a strong Acetaminophen. It was..." He glanced at his watch. "About five hours ago. Likely not in my system any longer."

She nodded. "Okay."

"Plus, I'm not driving today."

She halted, then kept moving. His brows rose in the air. "What was that?"

"I have a showing at the condos tonight with Layton Terry."

Mason's head went back. "Oh. Shit. I'm sorry. I forgot."

She grinned. "It's perfectly understandable. You've had a day."

"Skip the beer. What are you having?"

"Iced tea."

"I'll have the same, please."

She turned to the fridge and pulled the pitcher of tea from inside. Standing next to Mason, she poured tea into his glass, then repeated for her glass. His arm wrapped around her waist, and he squeezed her. "I'm sorry. I should have remembered."

Carley chuckled. "I'm not mad or sad. It's perfectly fine. I don't expect you to come with me. You have a hole in your leg."

He shook his head. "I have a dent in my leg, not a hole. It's little more than that."

She chuckled, kissed the top of his head, then sat across from him. "So we have a green salad, and cheesy broccoli and chicken casserole."

"It smells amazing."

He used the spoon she'd put on the table to dish himself a healthy portion. She smiled as he ate. He nodded often and hummed his appreciation. "This is really good."

It felt good to cook for someone who appreciated their food and enjoyed your cooking.

Mason carried his plate to the sink. Carley stood with her plate, "I can get that. You should sit down and rest."

He chuckled. "I'm good, Carley. It's a little sore, and I still have a slight headache, but I'm good."

He helped her clear the table. She filled the dishwasher, and he put the leftover casserole into a storage container. She looked at her watch, and he knew she was worried about the showing.

"Hey, why don't you drop me off at the Sandbar and I'll follow you to the condos. I'll have my truck back and it'll save Jace and Margo from having to run it over."

"Okay."

"Are you nervous about the showing?"

She smiled and he enjoyed staring at her. She was something special. His heart thumped in his chest. "A little apprehensive, I guess."

He wrapped his arms around her and pulled her in for a hug. "I'm sorry. This is the downside of being a real estate mogul."

She laughed into his chest and the vibration of it rippled through his body.

"Or a real estate agent."

He squeezed her tighter. "Don't sell yourself short."

She giggled into his chest, and he closed his eyes. She was getting past his walls. His heartbeat became erratic, and his breathing grew uneven.

She stepped back. "Are you alright?"

"Yeah."

He turned and stepped from the kitchen. "Are you ready to go or do you need some time?"

"I'm ready." She quickly moved to the counter and packed her laptop away, grabbed her purse, and met him near the door to the garage.

He opened the door and let her pass him, then he gently stepped out onto the top step and forced himself to use his leg to step down so it didn't stiffen up. He ground his teeth together so he wouldn't grimace. It wasn't as bad as he expected.

Carley waited to make sure he didn't need help. He was glad he didn't. He opened her door and waited until she was situated in the seat before closing it. He moved a bit slower than he usually would around the vehicle and slowly climbed into the passenger side.

Carley glanced down at his leg, then her eyes slid up to his. "Okay?"

"Yeah."

She nodded then tapped the garage door opener and waited a minute for the door to finish going up before she backed out. Closing the door as she moved onto the street, he took in the entire house from the street. He hadn't noticed it much when they'd arrived.

"It's a beautiful house."

She smiled and looked at it for a moment. "It is a beautiful home. But it's a bit lonely. I was thinking I needed to get a dog."

He smiled. "What kind of a dog would you get?"

"A Shepherd. Maybe a Malinois. Something that would intimidate anyone thinking of doing anything they shouldn't be doing."

He chuckled. "Good idea."

"Did you ever have a dog?"

He shook his head. He'd begged his parents for a dog growing up. "My parents never wanted the hassle of a dog. My mom didn't want the mess. My dad didn't want the expense. So, even though my brother and I begged for a dog. Every birthday and Christmas, we both asked. Every year we were denied."

"What about when you got out of the service?"

He watched the houses go by his window as a bit of sadness seeped in. "No. I worried about my PTSD and never really felt settled anywhere. Plus, I usually lived in apartments, and it's tough to find a place that will allow pets. So, I never got one. It would have been fun, though."

"Yeah. We always had a dog growing up. There are four of us girls and we had to take turns feeding them. Of course, in the beginning, we were so excited we'd be mad when it was someone else's turn to feed them. But as we grew up, it became a chore. But we loved the dogs we had. They loved us too."

He grinned. That sounded like an ideal childhood. Parents, kids, and dogs. "I suppose you lived in a perfect neighborhood like this."

She chuckled. "Not as nice as this. We were very middle class. Dad worked as an accountant. Mom worked part-time in a department store. We went to a decent school, the house was clean, and we had food and shelter."

"You had it all then."

She turned her head to look at him. "What about you?"

He took a deep breath. "We were on the lower level of middle class. Dad worked in a mill and Mom didn't work. When the mill closed down, Dad had a hard time finding work. We had lean years. He was a great carpenter, though, and eventually, he started his own handyman business. That business did well, and he'd bring my brother, Burke, and I with him as we got older. We learned to do things that were life skills. There's always something to fix or repair and I can do a fair amount of it. I'm lucky that way."

"Is that why you went into medicine?"

He shrugged. "I went into the Army. Took all the aptitude tests and tested well for the medical field. I liked the idea of helping people. So, I took that as my MOS."

She smiled. "That's wonderful. What a great calling."

It felt like a hot rock dropped into his stomach. He ended up not helping as many people as he'd hoped. Didn't they come to tell him each night how badly he'd failed?

Carley pulled into the lot at the Sandbar and pulled in next to his truck. She grinned at him, and he leaned in and kissed her lips. "See you in a few."

"Okay." She smiled at him, and he sat transfixed for a moment.

"You really are a beautiful woman, Carley Page."

She smiled and her eyes glistened. "Thank you."

He stared a bit longer. His stomach was tight. His heart felt as if it was filled with sand. He nodded and slowly got out of her SUV.

She waited for him to get into his truck. He managed it fairly well. Since his left leg was his wounded leg and he climbed in with his right leg, he managed a smooth entry. Glancing back at Carley, she smiled beautifully. It was ridiculous to feel proud about getting into a truck. But for some reason, the way she smiled at him made him feel pride. His dad would scoff at him for that. Since he was no longer around to tell him off about it, he'd never know.

Carley pulled out of the parking lot, and he followed behind her. As he neared the exit, Jace came out of the building. "Hey, how are you doing?"

He stopped and rolled his window down. It was beginning to get dusky, not dark yet, but not bright anymore. "I'm doing better. I had a nap and a meal. I'm feeling much stronger."

"Good. Take a couple of days off to recoup."

"Nah. I'll be in tomorrow."

Jace shook his head. "Are you kidding me? Take the days you need to heal."

He grinned. "I'm the doctor, Jace. I'm alright. How about I call you in the morning, and we'll chat about it?"

Jace drummed his hands on the window ledge of Mason's truck. "Sounds like a plan. Any word from your military contact?"

"Not yet. He said later today. I'll touch base with him in the morning if I don't hear from him. But he's prompt so he'll call today."

Jace nodded. "Sounds good. Talk to you tomorrow."

Mason nodded and waited for Jace to step away from his truck. He slowly pulled from the lot and drove to his new place.

Carley pulled into the parking area at the Barracks. There were three cars in the lot, all parked in the front row, but none of the cars looked like Layton Terry's.

She parked at the far end of the front row of the lot. It was actually closest to Mason's patio doors since he had the last unit on the first floor. Those units had the nice patio doors to the side yard. Once it was finished, at least.

She opened her door and stepped from her vehicle. She leaned back in to retrieve her purse and her folder with the Offer and Addendum form she'd need to write this offer. Layton said he'd be making an offer, so she wanted to be prepared and not have to run back to her vehicle. She stepped back and stood up to close her door when something was placed over her head. It took a few moments for her to realize what happened. Then panic set in. Dropping the papers in her hand, she grabbed at the cloth bag or pillowcase or whatever it was over her head. An arm wrapped around her waist, and she started kicking and screaming. A sharp poke near her neck scared her further. She began to feel woozy and her thoughts were jumbled. Her arms and legs felt as if they were made of lead, then there was nothing.

24

Mason drove up Main Street as darkness fell. It was funny how as soon as the sun began to set, darkness fell within minutes.

He pulled into the lot and saw Carley's SUV at the end of the first row, nearest his patio door. A grin spread on his face, and he marveled how in one moment he'd be afraid of disappointing her or feeling less than the man she deserved, to being so happy to just see her car in his lot. He shook his head. Weird.

His phone rang, and he looked at the readout. Ethan Dougherty.

Tapping the button on his phone, he sat in his truck and greeted his friend. "Hey, Ethan. Thanks for calling back."

"You're welcome, Mason. So, a couple of things. I'm sending Mitch DeMario to Blossom Springs to retrieve the thumb drive. Do you remember him?"

"I do. Is he still in the Marines?"

"Negative. He is in the security business, but he maintains clearances, and we hire him to do certain jobs for us."

"Okay. When should I expect him?"

"I believe he'll be there tomorrow. I've given him your number and he'll touch base with you on his ETA."

"Great. I'll wait to hear from him."

Ethan was quiet for a moment then his voice changed. "Is everything okay with you, Mason?"

Mason leaned his head back on the headrest and closed his eyes. "Yeah." He let out a deep breath. "PTSD got me. I struggled to perform surgery, so I quit. I kicked around a bit and remembered my brother, Burke, had come down here and had a great time, so I decided to check it out myself. I found a bartending gig in a beachfront bar. Great boss. Nice co-workers and pouring drinks doesn't give me panic attacks. Actually, I just bought a condo here which is a converted barracks."

"No kidding?"

"Weird. Right?"

"Different. But at least they're being used. The military has far too much waste in old buildings."

"Yeah. If you find yourself in need of sunshine and friendship, come on down and have a look. It would be great to see you."

Ethan chuckled. "That sounds like a plan. I'm getting married later this year. Maybe Christmas in Florida is on the books."

"I like it."

"Thanks for contacting me about the thumb drive. It was great talking to you."

"Ten-four. I hope to see you and the woman you've managed to dupe into marrying you soon."

Ethan's laugh was the last thing he heard before the call ended.

A sheet of paper blew past his truck, and his brows furrowed. Heaving out a breath, he stepped down from his truck and moved toward the paper. Just as he picked it up, another paper blew toward him. Grabbing that one, too, he looked down at the papers and saw they were real estate sheets. His head jerked back, and he moved toward Carley's SUV. He looked inside and saw the usual accordion file she carried with various real estate documents inside. She was neat and organized all the time. But she'd never let them blow out of her car.

He walked around the passenger side of the SUV and didn't see anything lying around. As he rounded the driver's side, his heart nearly stopped. Her purse lay on the ground, half under the vehicle. The brown folder she carried was also on the ground...he glanced at the documents in his hand and one was an Offer to Purchase.

His stomach twisted. He picked up her purse and the brown folder and then ran inside the building. "Carley."

He hurried down to Unit Five and twisted the handle. It was locked. "Carley?" He knocked on the door.

Fear. Real fear slammed into his chest and his breathing grew shallow. He could barely take a breath.

He pulled his phone out and tapped her number. His vision grayed and he leaned against the wall. He listened to her phone ring, and then the acid in his stomach multiplied when her purse rang. He closed his eyes. "Fuck!"

The door to Unit One opened. "What's going on here?"

"Call the police."

"What?"

Mason took a deep breath. "Please call the police. My girlfriend has been kidnap..." He swallowed and tried breathing. He couldn't say it. He shook his head. "She's gone."

The man, his neighbor, came to stand across the hall from him. Mason tried to listen as he felt the panic attack trying to take hold. His neighbor called the police, and Mason's shaking fingers tapped Jace's number.

"Hey, Mason, what's up?"

"She's gone. She's not..." He tried to breathe. "Carley... her car's here. Her purse and notebook were lying on the ground next to her car. She's not here." He sucked in a deep breath. "Panic. I'm hav..."

"Where are you?"

Mason struggled but managed to say, "Home."

"I'm on my way."

He pressed his back to the wall and felt his neighbor stand near him. "It's alright man. I'm here with you. How about we slide down the wall, so you don't fall?"

He felt like he was floating. The room came in and out of focus. His neighbor said, "My name is Asa. I just moved into Unit One. I get these attacks too."

Mason nodded once and rested his head back. Asa kept talking to him. Then he heard Jace's voice.

"Mason. It's Jace. Take a deep breath and when you're ready, take a sip of water."

More voices came toward him, and his breathing returned to near normal. His focus cleared, and he looked into Jace's eyes. "She's been taken. She's not here. Her purse and her files were on the ground by her car. We have to find her."

Jace looked around and saw the purse and files. He swallowed heavily and looked up at someone else. Mason turned his head to see Trey Fielding and a female officer standing in the hallway. Trey knelt down. "Can you tell me what happened?"

Mason told him what had happened as far as he knew it. Then he remembered... "Call Quinn Kurtz and see if he had the security system completed this week. We may have video."

Jace nodded. "Great thought." Jace stood. "Can you stand?"

Mason nodded. Jace held out his hand and pulled Mason up as much as he propelled himself up. He leaned against the wall and the officer with Trey held out her hand. My name is Erin Moody."

He shook her hand. She nodded, "How about if we go sit at one of the tables in the front and you can tell me again what happened?"

Mason nodded. He always felt tired after an attack, but wanted to be out looking for her. He followed Erin Moody to the common area. She motioned to a chair for him to sit and he shook his head. She smiled. "Please sit down."

He asked, "Did you find the man who put the note on her windshield the other day?"

Trey came and sat at the table as did Jace. Trey shook his head. "No, we weren't able to find him yet. Last we saw him was today when you got shot."

Erin turned her head to Trey, then said, "Oh." She opened her notebook, then looked him in the eye. "Okay, please tell me everything that happened."

25

Carley's mouth was dry. She tried moving her tongue around her mouth, but it felt like she'd swallowed a bag of sand. Dry and gritty and her tongue stuck to the roof of her mouth.

She opened her eyes; it took a few blinks to moisten them enough to open them. Once she'd managed it, all that met her was darkness. The room was dark. She couldn't see anything. There didn't seem to be a window or a sliver of light anywhere.

Her head felt like someone was hammering a nail into it. More than a dull pain, the back of her head throbbed.

She took slow, steady breaths. She needed to figure out where she was. She raised her right hand to rub her forehead, but it was stuck...She tugged to loosen it, but it was held tight. Tugging again, the binding bit into her skin, and she stopped. She tried to move her left arm, but it was also fastened, but to something around her waist. She tugged a few times. It was tightly fastened to a belt or something. Opening her fingers, she felt the device around her waist. About three inches wide, and it felt like material. A strap of some sort. Obviously, with rings or clips on it to secure her hands. The dread began filling her mind, and her breathing increased.

She moved her feet; they weren't tied. She was lying on a bed or a cot or something. She remembered the cloth covering her head, the prick in her neck, and her stomach twisted. Her heartbeat increased, and the horrible scenarios began playing in her mind. Where was she? Who took her? Why? Would she get out of here alive? She felt the tears sting her eyes. She closed them tightly, at least there was moisture in them now.

She listened for sounds. A radio, a television. Anything. It was eerily quiet wherever she was. She inhaled deeply and let it out slowly. Then she heard a sound. She froze and listened intently.

Footsteps.

Slowly coming toward her.

She held her breath until they stopped. The sound of a key scraping into a lock, then the click of it unlocking. She counted her breathing to keep it even. All the safety videos she'd watched over the years always said the same thing. Try to stay calm and think clearly.

The door opened and a sliver of light illuminated the room for a brief moment. She saw a chair and table near the door. The person neared her slowly, the footsteps were heavy and measured.

"You have something that belongs to me. I want it back."

She let out a breath. This again. This guy was a pain in the ass. She took a deep breath. "I gave it to the police."

"Don't lie to me."

"I'm not lying."

Her heartbeat increased, and she could feel panic rising in her stomach. She took a slow, measured breath and let it out slowly. She swallowed or tried to, but her mouth was still so dry.

"When?"

"Ah." She stopped and searched her mind. It was still slightly disoriented. When was that? "Two days ago. I think."

"Bullshit." The footsteps moved away then turned and came back. A chair scraped across the floor, at least it sounded like a chair. Then the squeak as he sat in it.

"Now, let's try this again. When did you give it to the police?"

She tried calming herself. Stay calm. Think. "I think about two days ago. I don't know. I gave it to my brother-in-law. He took it to the police."

Another squeak of the chair and she waited. Steady breaths. Stay calm. You can do this.

"Who's your brother-in-law?"

The pounding in her head increased. She tried swallowing again.

His voice deepened. "I'm waiting..."

She didn't want to give Jace up. She didn't want them in trouble. She didn't want her sister to be taken too. Her heartbeat increased and she felt the sweat between her breasts. She shouldn't have said as much as she did. She'd never make a good spy.

He leaned in closer. "Let me take a guess. I did some checking on you and found out you recently bought Price Realty from your sister, Margo Price...Marriott. How is that for some investigative work? So, I'm going to take a stab at this and say Jace Marriott has what belongs to me."

"He doesn't. He took it to the police."

"How do you know?"

"He told me."

"Well, I'm going to see about getting it back and if you're lying, you're going to pay for it."

Her stomach rolled. What did that mean? Scenarios ran through her head. None of them seemed good. For her at least. It was better not to worry about it.

A finger slid down her bare arm, from her shoulder to her wrist. Slowly sliding the length of her arm. Then his finger traced her collarbone slowly, and her breathing hitched and came in shallow spurts. She closed her eyes. She couldn't see anything anyway. Praying he wouldn't do anything awful, she tried pushing the thoughts from her head as they threatened to plant themselves in her mind. His finger then slid across her forehead and down her temple. "You're beautiful."

Her stomach tossed and she thought she'd vomit her casserole up. "Can I have some water?"

He removed his hand from her face and sat still for a moment. Then she heard the cap of a water bottle twist, and he held it to her lips. She was lying down and tried lifting her head to drink, but she was in an awkward position, so the water rolled down her cheek and onto the bed. He pulled it away and recapped the bottle. At least she managed some water. Her throat felt better.

He stood abruptly and walked across the room. She turned her eyes in the direction of his footsteps and held her breath. As soon as the door opened, light shone into the room. She managed to glance down at her hand to see what it was tied to. It looked like the springs of a bed. She might be able to use a sawing motion and cut the zip ties. Her left hand didn't have a lot of room to move at all. She'd focus on her right hand.

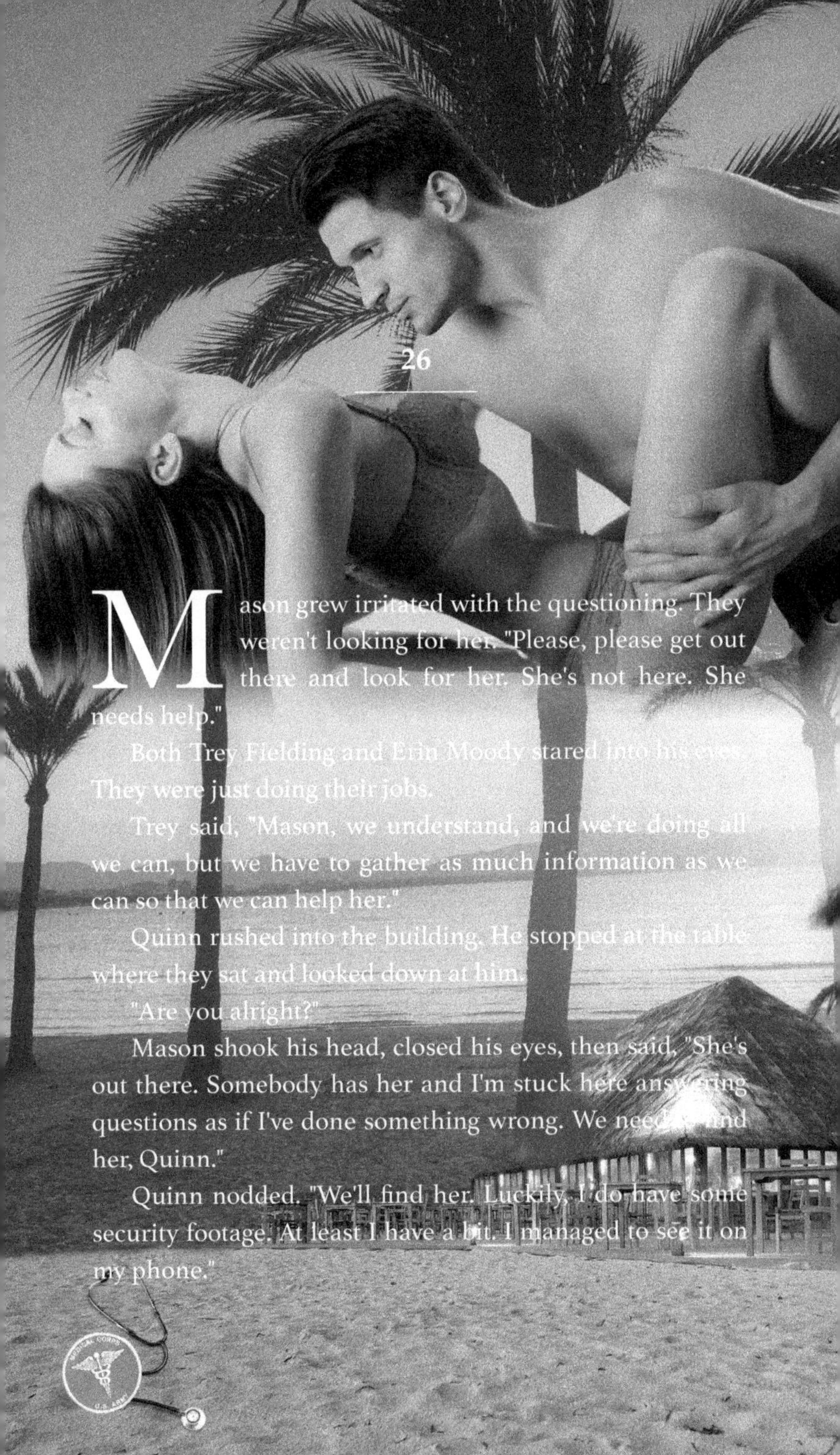

26

Mason grew irritated with the questioning. They weren't looking for her. "Please, please get out there and look for her. She's not here. She needs help."

Both Trey Fielding and Erin Moody stared into his eyes. They were just doing their jobs.

Trey said, "Mason, we understand, and we're doing all we can, but we have to gather as much information as we can so that we can help her."

Quinn rushed into the building. He stopped at the table where they sat and looked down at him.

"Are you alright?"

Mason shook his head, closed his eyes, then said, "She's out there. Somebody has her and I'm stuck here answering questions as if I've done something wrong. We need to find her, Quinn."

Quinn nodded. "We'll find her. Luckily, I do have some security footage. At least I have a bit. I managed to see it on my phone."

He motioned to Trey Fielding. If you follow me, the security closet is over here. Mason got up to go but was halted by Officer Moody. "I'm sorry you have to stay here with me."

"I want to see. I might be able to help. I might know the person. I might be able to identify him."

"In due time," she responded. "First, let Chief Fielding see what he can see."

Frustrated, Mason sat back in the chair. "This is ridiculous."

It wasn't long before Chief Fielding and Quinn came back into the room.

Mason sat up straighter. "Can I see? Did you see him? Did you see somebody? Do you know who it is?"

Quinn glanced at Trey and then back to Mason. "We can see a man. He's wearing a dark jacket. His hair is lighter. Military cut. He was sitting in his car a couple of cars away from where Carley parked. He got out as she was digging her paperwork from her car. He caught her by surprise. And it looked like he injected her with something. We don't have his face, though. I don't know if he realized that there was a camera watching the parking lot or if it was dumb luck on his part. But she was definitely taken."

Mason's stomach turned. What to do now? What if she needed him and what did he inject her with? Things started running through his mind. The different drugs that would render somebody unconscious or unable to move. "She might need medical help. We don't know what he injected her with."

Chief Fielding nodded. "Yes, we've taken that into consideration but first before we can do anything else we need to find her."

"So what do you have to go on?"

We have the car on camera. We managed to get the plate number, and I've called it in. Blossom Springs PD is running it now. I've called in the state police. We're running the photographs of the car, the plates, and his picture through the database. Hopefully, someone will be able to identify him. But in the meantime, we'll be patrolling, and so will state and county police. Do you have any other questions?"

Mason's breathing was ragged and measured. His hands shook slightly. He picked up the water bottle Jace had brought him and took a healthy drink. She needed help. She needed someone to help her. This all seemed slow and agonizing.

Then he blurted out, "So we're supposed to just sit here and wait and hope that you see a car driving by? What if he's already got her somewhere?"

"Mason, we know this is difficult. Believe me, we know, and we're doing the best we can. We have protocol we have to follow, and we're doing everything we can to move as expeditiously as possible."

Mason swallowed. His eyes moved to Jace who sat alongside quietly. His jaw was tense as if he was gritting his teeth. That gave Mason some comfort at least. Jace cared as much as he did. At least somebody else was also irritated with the slow process.

Police officers left and Mason turned to Jace. "We have to do something. We have to do something to help her."

"I agree. Do you have thoughts?"

"I do, actually. I have a friend, Mitch DeMario, who is in the security business. He's going to be in town soon to pick up the thumb drive from you. I want to bring him in since he'll be in town anyway. I want him to help with this. Before you give him the thumb drive, let's talk to him."

Mason's phone rang and he quickly grabbed it off the table hoping Carley had managed to get to a phone.

Jace said, "Answer it, Mason. What if it's the kidnapper?"

Mason tapped the answer call icon and put it on speaker. "Mason Thompson."

"Hey, Mason, it's Mitch DeMario. I'm fifteen minutes away from Blossom Springs. Ethan Dougherty gave me your phone number. I'm not sure if you remember who I am; we serve..."

Mason interrupted him. "I know exactly who you are. Listen, Mitch, I'm sorry to throw you into this so abruptly, but my girlfriend was kidnapped about an hour ago. I could really use your help on this. It's gonna take the police forever while they're following protocol. We have some video footage, a visual of the vehicle, a plate number, and that's about it. We could sure use your help."

Mitch was quiet for a moment. When he responded, Mason felt immediately relieved. "Okay, well, I'm sorry to hear that first of all, but it's a good thing that you have some video footage. Where can I meet you, and what are we doing?"

"I'm at the Barracks Condos at the end of Main Street. When you get to Blossom Springs turn down Main Street and head all the way to the end. Main Street actually ends in our parking lot. I'm here with Jace Marriott and Quinn Kurtz. Quinn is the developer of these condos, and he has the video footage here."

"Ten-four. I'll be there in just under 15 minutes."

Mason stood and took in some deep breaths. He felt stronger now than he had in a long time. "Okay, so here's what I propose. We're gonna get Mitch here and we'll get that video cued up so he can see what you have. We're gonna work this our way. The way we would do in the military when we're looking for someone. The way we know how. That's what we're gonna do."

Quinn turned his eyes toward Jace.

Jace to his credit, didn't patronize him or say anything other than, "I'm with you. Let's do this."

arley wiggled her hand back and forth on the bedspring, hoping that she could wear the zip tie down or break it completely. It bit into her wrist, and she could feel the moisture as her wrist started to bleed. But she was so worried about what else might happen if she stayed where she was.

That stupid medallion, why did she ever pick the damn thing up to begin with? She should have just left it there in the closet. But then again, Mason bought that condo, and this guy would be after Mason. Though he wouldn't have been able to pick him up and carry Mason away as easily as he carried her.

She continued to work her arm back and forth, back and forth, back and forth, praying the entire time, "Please God, please let me get loose, please let me get loose, please let me get loose."

She heard the key in the door, and she froze. She whispered to calm herself, "He's back, he's back, he's back. What am I going to do?"

She hoped he wouldn't look at her wrist and see it was

bleeding. The door opened and he stepped inside and closed the door, rendering the room dark once again.

The slow measured steps coming toward her made her eyes tear up. Even breaths, she told herself slowly.

"Even breaths," she whispered again.

He sat in the chair, it creaked slightly. It creaked again and she felt the heat from his body as he moved closer to her. Her emotions battled between feeling like she was going to vomit, to feeling complete and total fear.

She swallowed and waited. "It looks like your brother-in-law has been a busy duck. I don't like busy ducks. Do you understand me? I don't like them at all." He moved closer, his breath brushed over her cheek. "There's people milling about his business. They're at the back door, the front door, everywhere. Police are combing the parking lot, so I couldn't get near. Tell me this, Carley Page, if your brother-in-law gave my property to the police, why would the police be at his place?"

Her mind raced. She didn't know. How would she know?

"I don't know. Obviously, I'm here, not there. I don't know what's going on."

"I think you're lying to me is what I think. I think you're holding out on me, and I don't like it."

She swallowed the large lump in her throat. He sounded as if he was getting angry. Probably wasn't a good idea to make him angry.

"I don't know what's going on. I'm guessing the police are there because they know I'm missing, and that it has nothing to do with your property. But that would just be a guess."

He sat back. She could hear the rustling of his clothes. He wore some sort of material that made noise. Like a ski jacket or something.

"Well, I guess my next step will be to go talk to someone else that might know something. Maybe your sister."

A sob broke out Carley's throat. She didn't mean for it to, but it did. "Please, please don't bother her. Please don't. Please leave my sister alone. Please. Please leave my sister alone." She begged.

"Well, if her husband has something that belongs to me, she and I are going to have a problem. And if she confirms her husband actually did turn my property over to the police, I'm going to have to move on to Plan B or C. Someone's not telling me the truth somewhere along the way and that bothers me. Plus, if I have your sister, I can trade her for my property."

"I'm telling you the truth. I swear it." She swallowed, "I gave it to Jace. Jace gave it to the police. I don't know what else to tell you. I don't have what you're looking for. I don't have it. I gave it to Jace."

"Well, we'll see about that. If Jace has it, I'm sure your sister knows where it's at. Maybe a gun to her head will help her locate what I'm looking for."

She sobbed, and her body shook. He got up abruptly and moved toward the door. He slammed the door behind him, sliding the key into the lock once again. She listened as his footsteps faded away.

She started sawing madly at the zip tie on her wrist. She needed to get out of here.

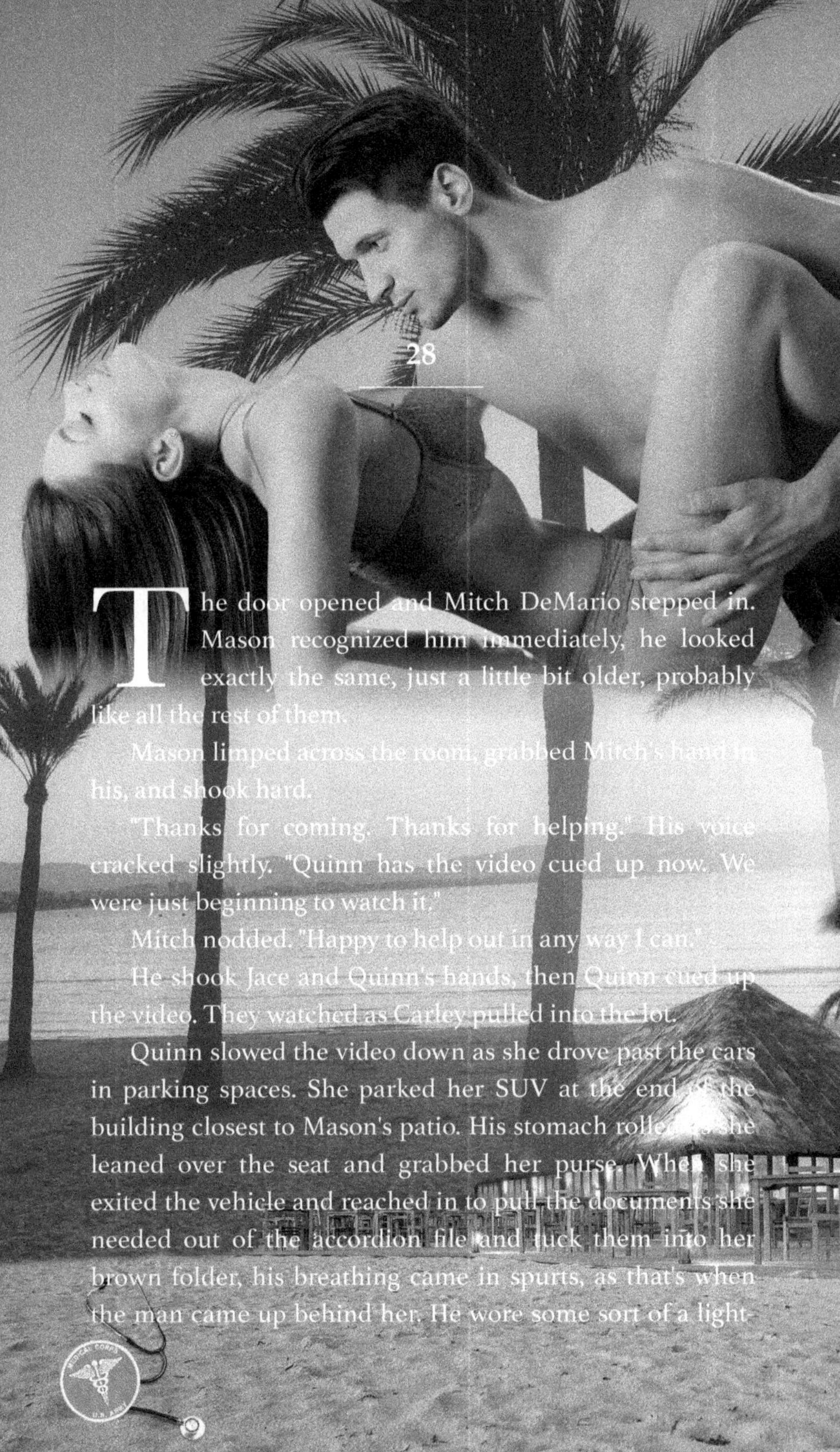

28

The door opened and Mitch DeMario stepped in. Mason recognized him immediately, he looked exactly the same, just a little bit older, probably like all the rest of them.

Mason limped across the room, grabbed Mitch's hand in his, and shook hard.

"Thanks for coming. Thanks for helping." His voice cracked slightly. "Quinn has the video cued up now. We were just beginning to watch it."

Mitch nodded. "Happy to help out in any way I can."

He shook Jace and Quinn's hands, then Quinn cued up the video. They watched as Carley pulled into the lot.

Quinn slowed the video down as she drove past the cars in parking spaces. She parked her SUV at the end of the building closest to Mason's patio. His stomach rolled as she leaned over the seat and grabbed her purse. When she exited the vehicle and reached in to pull the documents she needed out of the accordion file and tuck them into her brown folder, his breathing came in spurts, as that's when the man came up behind her. He wore some sort of a light weight ski jacket, dark, long-sleeved, which in itself was weird. It was nearly eighty-nine degrees outside today. He pulled what looked like a pillowcase or hood from his pocket and shoved it over Carley's head.

She began squirming, kicking, fighting. He grabbed a syringe from his pocket and injected her at the back of her neck. Mason wanted to throw up just watching that. His heart raced, and his knees shook slightly. What was she going through right now? He dragged her over to one of the cars in the parking lot and tossed her in the back seat haphazardly. Her body was limp as a rag, and he could see her bounce as he tossed her in. He jumped in the driver's seat and as he backed the car up, Mason said, "Stop!"

They looked closely into the camera, and you could see his face, though it was shadowed and certainly not a clear picture.

Mason said, "I know who that is. I know who that is."

Jace looked at him. "Well, who is it? Does he know her? How would he know she was going to be here?"

"He's been here before. That's Layton Terry, a client she was here to meet. She didn't like him an said he gave her a bad vibe. I asked her to wait until I got here to show him the place. She was likely going to come inside and wait."

Mitch DiMario stepped closer to the camera and stared at Layton Terry's face. "How many times has she met him before?"

"Once that I'm aware of. That was yesterday. That was when she found the thumb drive you're here to get. The landscapers were out front digging and putting in plants. As she stood there with Layton Terry, she found the thumb drive in the fresh dirt and picked it up. He seemed terribly interested in it. She just said, 'Well, Quinn Kurtz owns this place, so I'll give it to Quinn. He can decide what to do with it.' Terry insisted on seeing it a few times, and then I stepped in. Told him it was hers to do with as she wanted, and she was right. Quinn Kurtz was the owner of these condos, and he would be the one to take possession of the thumb drive. Terry didn't seem especially pleased with that explanation, so I'm guessing that's when he devised this plan."

Mitch's brows furrowed. "Why didn't he just grab it and run?"

Mason let out a deep breath. "I'm quite a bit bigger than he is. He probably didn't think that he could take me or outrun me, so he devised this plan instead."

Mitch glanced at him and sized him up. He must have felt satisfied with the explanation.

Mitch grinned. "I can see that. Okay, keep rolling the video. Let's see what else happens."

Quinn replied, "Not much else happens here. He drives out of sight and then off he goes."

Mitch nodded. "Okay, so the first thing we have to do is run Layton Terry through the system. Did police see this?"

Quinn responded, "Yeah, they saw it, but they wouldn't let Mason in while they were viewing it,, so he wasn't able to identify Terry for them."

"I see. Okay, so I'll contact the local police and tell them we have a possible ID. Let them know who we're looking for and see if they'll help us out by running some reports on Terry's address and any properties he might have here or close to town. How about in the meantime, while the police are doing that, I retrieve the thumb drive from you and see what's on it. It might help us determine what he's after."

Jace nodded. "Okay, that sounds good. Let's go. It's at my restaurant. Carley is my wife's sister, and I haven't told her yet what's happened. I'm gonna need to speak with her for a couple of minutes before we go storming in there making all kinds of plans."

Mitch glanced at Mason.

Mason said, "Why don't you go now, Jace, and let Margo know? We'll be right behind you."

"Okay, thanks." Jace quickly left the building.

Mitch addressed Quinn. "Can I get a copy of this video?"

"Sure, I'll make it right now. I emailed one to the police."

"Why don't you do that for me too? Email it to me. I'll have it on my phone whenever I need it."

"Okay." Quinn tapped a couple of keys on the computer.

Mason felt a bit better, but not much. He still wanted to know she was safe. He wanted her back and he didn't want it to take too much longer. She was in danger and that thought made him sick.

29

Carley felt the zip tie around her wrist loosen. She swallowed as her blood raced. Just a few more scrapes and, hopefully, she would be free. At least this much of it, anyway. She worked a little harder at the zip tie, scraping it back and forth, hoping it was working. The sooner the better.

She felt it loosen, then she heard a little pop, and she lifted her arm. She was free. She was free at least from being tied to the bed. She sat up slowly and tried to think things through. She couldn't make a mistake.

The bed creaked slightly as she moved. Those old bedsprings squeaked every time a person moved. It was a wonder anyone got sleep back in the day. She sat up, took a deep breath, and slowly stood. She gave herself a moment to make sure her balance was fine. She held her right hand out in front of her. Her left hand was still attached to the belt on her waist. With her right hand, she felt around the belt for a buckle, a tie, or a fastener. She slid her hand from the front to where her left hand was fastened all the way around to the back. There it was! She felt it. It was a buckle of some sort. She tried feeling for the end of the rope to see if she could pull it through the ring of the buckle, but there didn't seem to be a ring. She pressed her fingertips against the buckle, and it was a square metal buckle or fastener. She felt slowly around the fastener and then felt the lip of the latch. She pulled it forward with her forefinger, and it released the belt around her waist. "Oh," she gasped.

She almost cried. It felt so good, her blood began rushing to all of her limbs, and though it tingled and pricked, she was free. She let her arm hang down for a moment. Looking at the fastener, she didn't know how she was going to remove the belt from her wrist. It looked like a handcuff. It was a metal something attaching her hand to the belt.

She swallowed and counted her blessings, at least she was free. She gathered the belt so she didn't make noise or hook it on anything. She bundled it up in her left hand.

Slowly, she moved around the room. What was here that she could use as a weapon? There had to be something. She found a dresser against the wall near the foot of the bed. She slowly ran her hands along the top of the dresser. She found something firm. She felt the object with her fingers. It felt like an old hurricane lamp. She continued along the dresser; she needed a weapon. Next to the lamp was a glass dish of some sort. She continued, then halted. She went back to the lamp. Could she turn it on? She felt for some sort of a switch, a knob, a toggle, anything.

Not finding anything on the lamp she reached for the cord to see if there was a little switch on the cord. She found it.

Her finger bumped into it. She turned it on. The light was low and not nearly enough to light the entire room.

Only one bulb seemed to work, and that was in the bottom globe, but it gave her something.

Reminding herself to stay calm, she took a couple of calming breaths and slowly looked around the room as her eyes adjusted to the dimness. The glass bowl was sitting on the old-fashioned dresser. It had cowboys or some kind of Western scene carved on the front. Then she halted.

She knew this house. Oh my god, she knew where she was. Her blood raced through her body, and adrenaline flowed. She looked around, feeling more alert. If she remembered correctly, there was a closet at the end of the dresser. She slowly moved to the closet. The door was an accordion door. She slowly slid it open, trying so hard not to make any noise at all. Once it was pushed open, she looked inside for anything that she could use as a weapon. Anything. A bat. Anything.

She found some pieces of wood that had been cut to make something and were then discarded. Picking up one of them, she was happy to see that one end was cut at a forty-five-degree angle, so it had a little bit of a point. She didn't want to stab anybody with an old, dirty piece of wood, but she was going to do it to save her life.

She edged herself over to the door and waited. She tried the handle. It was locked firmly. From this side of the door, there was no lock on it to turn and open. In the dim light, she saw the gleam on the handle and lock. It was new; somebody had changed the lock and the knob recently.

Then she heard footsteps. She hurried back to the lamp and turned the light off, then as quickly as she could without making noise, she moved herself over to the door. Her heart hammered so hard in her chest, and her breathing was shallow. She tried to quiet her breathing and gripped the piece of wood with both hands. The sound of the metal key inserted into the lock had her heart racing. The knob turned on the door, and it opened with her behind it. The man stepped inside the room. She hesitated.

Could she actually stab him? She didn't know if she could do it. She changed her grip quietly on the board so she held it more like a bat. As soon as he was clear of the open door, she stepped out, reared back, and swung as hard as she could. Thud!

She hit him hard by the neck and he dropped to his knees. She hit him again and again. Then she hit him one last time and quickly bolted out the door.

30

Mason drove a little faster than he should have, but he was eager to get to the Sandbar and see what was on that thumb drive. Something important was on it or it wouldn't have garnered Carley's, or anyone's kidnapping. Mitch DeMario was behind him.

As soon as Mason threw his truck in park, he hopped out and winced when he tightened his thigh muscle where he'd been shot. He'd forgotten about that. All that was important right now was finding Carley.

He limped slightly toward the Sandbar.

DeMario caught up to him. "What's going on with the limp?"

"I got shot today."

"What?"

"Yeah, an officer's bullet ricocheted off a rock and hit me. It didn't go deep. It was actually not in far at all, and EMTs were able to pull it out."

"Holy shit, you're leading an exciting life here."

"To be honest with you, it's more exciting than I would

like right now. I just want to get my girlfriend back, spend time with her, do my job, and have a nice life with her."

"Okay, well let's see what we can do."

They hustled in the back door. Jace had pulled the thumb drive from the safe. Margo sat at her desk wiping her eyes. The second she saw him, she jumped up and hugged him.

"Oh, Mason, I can't believe this. I can't believe this. I just can't believe this."

"I know, Margo. We're going to get her back and we're going to do it as quickly as we can. I don't doubt the police are doing everything they can, but they're blocked by laws and rules. We aren't. Well, we are, but we're not."

Jace handed Mitch the thumb drive.

Mitch looked it over, turned it around in his hand, and nodded.

"Yeah, this is military grade for sure." He put it in Jace's computer then pulled his phone out and tapped a number.

"Hey, Ethan, it's Mitch. So I'm here in Blossom Springs, and we have a little bit of a snag. Carley Page, the woman who found the thumb drive, has been kidnapped. I'm here with Mason Thompson and friends. I want to see what's on the thumb drive to see if it can help us identify who has her. I need login information."

He listened, clicked on the logo, and the password and username screen popped up.

"Okay, go ahead. I have that screen open now."

He was given information to unlock the thumb drive and as soon as he clicked enter, the screen filled with infor-mation. He read it over, as Mason watched over his shoulder.

Mitch whistled a low, slow whistle. "This is information on Russia. It looks like secrets were being passed between the US and Russia regarding government equipment, including weapon diagrams.

He kept clicking back and forth between screens.

"Somebody's passing military secrets," Mitch said. "Hang on. I'm going to put you on speaker." He tapped the speaker icon on his phone.

"Mason Thompson, Jace Marriott, Quinn Kurtz, and Jace Marriott's wife, Margo are here with me."

He set his phone on the desk. "All right, folks, I have Ethan Dougherty here on the line."

"Hi, folks. I'm sorry about all that's happened there, but I'll help in any way I can." He took a deep breath. "All right, Mitch, click on the upper left corner. There's an icon there. Click on that."

Mitch did as he was told. "Done."

"All right, there's a number in there. Give me that number."

Mitch read off the number. In the background, you could hear the typing of keys.

Ethan then said. "That thumb drive has been missing for about a year."

Mitch stood up. "Well, what do you make of that?"

Ethan replied, "Where did you find it?"

Mitch looked over at Mason. "Hey, Ethan, it's Mason. Carley was speaking to landscapers outside the Barracks Condos last night. I told you about the condos yesterday. That's where I live. Landscapers are planting shrubbery around the building. As they were scraping the dirt into a hole, she saw the shine of the thumb drive and picked it up. She asked the landscapers if they'd dropped it, and they said no. I asked the landscaper if anything else had been uncovered. And he showed me a box that had been with it. I gave that box to Jace also."

Jace turned around and grabbed the box from the safe and handed it to Mitch. "I have the box here. Ethan, hang on. Let me look it over."

He turned the box all around. "It just seems to be a plain box with no writing or information on it of any sort. The drive was likely put into the box to protect it if someone buried it. Or to camouflage what was inside. Nothing denoting anything on it. I'll send pictures."

Mitch snapped pictures with his phone of the box and the drive, just for evidence sake. He tapped the photos and set his phone down.

"I've just sent them to you."

"Thanks," Ethan replied. "Okay, what I have here on my system is that along with that thumb drive, we are missing two others. The serial numbers are similar, and they went missing at the same time. But what I can also tell you is the information that you have on that thumb drive is needed for the other two thumb drives to mean anything. It's a newer system we have in place. These thumb drives were stolen from a secured storage locker. It'll take me a while to know if the information on them was overwritten or altered. They could have been stolen for the encryption. Or..." He took a deep breath. "Or this is an inside job, and we have a spy in our midst stealing information. I'll know more once I can match up the initial information uploaded to the drives and what you've found on it now."

Mitch took a deep breath and stood up. He looked over at Mason and shook his head.

Ethan asked, "Do you have any leads on the victim?"

Mitch cleared his throat, "Yeah, we have one. We're going to work on that right now. Do you have anyone listed as having checked those drives out?"

"Negative. They were stored by the locker commander and not checked out. That was fifteen months ago."

"Okay. Thanks." Mitch turned to Mason. "Anything?"

Ethan began talking before Mason could respond. "Also, I might also tell you that we have been following some individuals who are suspected of stealing military secrets. Two of them were caught about three months ago. Two of them remain at large."

Mason leaned forward, "Do you have the names of those two individuals at large?"

"Hang on, let me see." More keys were clacking.

Ethan came back with, "Affirmative. The two are Terry Bryan and Dustin Carter."

That didn't mean anything to him. He'd never heard of those people. He looked at Jace and Quinn. They both shook their heads.

Mitch said, "Thank you, Ethan. I'll be in touch. You do the same, please."

"Ten-four."

31

C arley ran up the stairs. She tripped a couple of times and stubbed her toes once, but she kept going. Fear propelled her faster than her legs ever could.

She reached the top of the stairs and heard a television or radio. Then she heard a chair squeak.

She froze. There was someone else up here. She hadn't counted on that. She thought there was just one person. She pressed her back against the wall and listened intently. She was in the kitchen. The sound seemed to come from the living room. Lucky for her, she remembered this house. She stepped to her left quietly and ducked around the corner to a mudroom. Beyond the mudroom was the door to the outside. She'd run down the road as fast as she could if she had to. She'd prefer a vehicle.

A voice called out, "Did she tell you anything?"

She froze. She didn't recognize the voice at all. It sounded menacing. Her heart hammered in her chest. She took some breaths and tried to hold them in to calm herself. The last thing she needed to do was to pass out from hyper ventilating. She swallowed and kept herself pressed tightly against the wall. The voice said again, "Did she tell you anything?"

She heard the chair squeak and then she heard him stalk across the living room floor. He hollered down the stairs. "Did she tell you anything?"

No sound came. He swore, "Fuck." He stomped down the stairs, and that was her chance. She tried the back door, but it was locked. She fumbled with the lock and twisted the old thing. Opening it, she found the deadbolt engaged. She gripped it as tightly as she could, twisted the knob, and unlocked the deadbolt. She slipped out the door and closed it quietly behind her. Hopefully, they wouldn't know which direction she went.

There were two vehicles in the driveway. She ran to both of them. Neither one had keys in it. Of course, they wouldn't leave keys in the cars, but she knew where she was. She took off running down the road. There was another house within just half of a block. She ran as fast as she could to that house and prayed somebody would be home. She made it to the house and ran around to the back door so she wouldn't be spotted. She was grateful there was no fence to have to hop.

She climbed the two back steps and started pounding on the door. "Hello, anybody, can you help me? Can you help me? I need help. Help." She kept pounding.

Finally, a dog started barking, and she closed her eyes. At least if somebody was in there, they would hear her now. And finally, an older gentleman came shuffling to the back door. He looked out the window and saw her.

She looked into his eyes. "Please help me. Please help me."

He opened the door as quickly as he could. Not nearly

quickly enough for her. And as soon as he opened the door, she pushed herself inside. "Please lock the door. Quickly."

She stood against the wall trying to catch her breath. When he'd locked the door, he turned to her.

"What do you need help with? Are you hurt?"

"I need you to call the police immediately. Please call the police. I was kidnapped. I just broke free. I was at Douglas Sanders's house. He's not there, and he didn't kidnap me, but that's where they were holding me."

"Doug Sanders? He...he's just next door."

"Yes, please call the police. Please."

The old man shook his head. Stuck his wrinkled hand in his pants pocket and pulled his phone out. He dialed 911 and put the phone to his ear.

It felt like an eternity before someone answered, but she could hear the operator's voice over the speaker. "911, what's your emergency?"

"My name is Jonathan Roberts, and I have a girl here who said she was kidnapped and was being held at the Douglas Sanders residence. But she's here now inside and we have the door locked but we need someone to come out please."

As soon as she heard the operator say we have someone en route Carley could have cried. She closed her eyes and leaned her head against the wall. Tears flowed immediately. Tears of joy, fear, relief. She wasn't sure which it was, but tears, nonetheless.

And then she heard Jonathan say, "Well, I'll be damned, there's two men walking through my backyard right now."

She gasped and looked out the window. "It's them they're looking for me. Oh my god. Please get the police here now."

"Okay, will do," he said. He held the phone to his ear. He said to her, "The operator said we're supposed to go deeper in the house so that we can stay hidden." She moved with Jonathan into his house. She was grateful not to be tied to a bed. "Here, why don't you sit at the dining room table here? I'll get you a cup of tea."

"No, I don't need anything. It's okay, I just want the police to come."

Carley was so afraid to look out the window, but she was even more afraid not to. She needed to be prepared. The man sat on a chair at the table, and she moved to the window. She stood alongside it and peered out, trying to stay as hidden as possible. Jonathan still had the 911 operator on his phone. He tapped the speaker button, and the operator said, "Mr. Roberts, are you still there with me?"

"Yes, we're here. We moved away from the back door and into the dining room."

"All right, the officers tell me they're close."

The faint sound of sirens could be heard, and Carley said, "I hear them! I hear them!" She fought back a sob and peered out the window for the two men.

Jonathan told the operator, "We can hear the sirens."

"Stay on with me, sir, until we're sure that they're there and they have found you."

"Okay." Carley continued to peer out the window. She held her hand over her stomach and that's when Jonathan gasped.

"She's got a rope tied around her hand."

Carley looked down and realized how that probably looked to him. She wasn't lying when she told them she'd been kidnapped.

A knock on the front door made Carley gasp.

Jonathan got up, "It's probably the police."

"No, don't open it," Carley yelled, but it was too late.

He opened the door. "Can I help you?"

That's when the man looked past Jonathan and right into her eyes. She was frozen for a moment, then fear took hold, and she bolted to the back door. She heard a crash, and deep in her mind, she hoped Jonathan wasn't hurt, but she knew if they caught her, she likely would be.

She swung the back door open and ran around the front of the house, trying to remember if there was another house close by. She saw a truck coming down the road and nearly cried. Hopefully, they could get her out of here and to safety.

A sharp burning pain seared through her shoulder, and then the sound of a gun rang in her ears.

32

Mitch turned to Mason, and just before he was about to say something, his phone rang. He pulled it up and his brows rose into his hair.

He looked at Mason as he answered his phone. "Hey Ethan."

Mitch stepped closer to Mason. Mason leaned in; he didn't want to miss a single word.

"I just received some intelligence, and I thought it might help you over there. Mason, are you close by?"

"Yes, I'm here."

Ethan continued. "All right, listen up. It appears that Terry Bryan also goes by the name Terry Layton and most recently Layton Terry. It was just confirmed through TSA, that he boarded a plane and landed in Tampa a week ago. Not saying that this is your guy, but I'm saying a man with some aliases near the same town as you, and also on our suspect list, would be someone very important to watch for. I don't have any information that he's checked into a hotel. We are checking that though, and I'll let you know as soon as I have something."

Mitch responded, "Thanks, Ethan. That's great information about the man Mason believes has Carley. I'll keep you posted. Out."

The call ended, and Mitch glanced at Mason. "We're gonna find her. We're getting close. But we don't have a location to search. We can ask the police to contact local businesses and look at their security cameras. He may show up on them, driving by or in the parking area. We can create a timeline with that information. We have a car, and we have a name. And we know he's not far from here because he wants the drive. We have that. And if he's the man trading military secrets for money, he wants what we have."

Mason's mind raced. "Then let's let him know we have it."

Mitch cocked his head. Jace and Quinn both straightened their posture.

Mitch said, "What do you mean?"

Mason replied, "I mean, we need to get the word out quickly that we found a military-grade thumb drive and it's here."

Mitch nodded. Jace sprang into action. "Well, the quickest way to do that would be through a couple of channels. We have the local radio station which is where I get the word out when I need something quickly. It was how we got the word out about Grace's petition signing, and we reached hundreds of people that night. And if he's monitoring social media, and/or police channels, we can get the word out on both of those."

"Okay," Mitch responded.

Mason nodded, "Yeah. Yeah, that sounds good let's start there. I'll do social media. Jace, you call the radio station. Mitch, you call local PD and ask them to broadcast across their radios and their scanners that there's a military-grade thumb drive found, and for right now, it's being held at the Sandbar."

Quinn said, "Well, wait a minute. Shouldn't we tell them it's at the police station? Why would having it here be bigger bait?"

Mason grinned, "Because they won't think there's security here."

Quinn nodded. "Gotcha. Okay. Great thinking, Mason."

They split up to go their separate ways. Mason quickly pulled up the Sandbar's social media page and made a new post. All capital letters.

"ANNOUNCEMENT. MILITARY GRADE THUMB DRIVE FOUND. Red in color. Stainless steel casing. A few scratches and bruises on it. Dug up by landscapers at the Barracks Condos. Being held at the Sandbar for safekeeping. If anyone knows who this belongs to, or if it's yours, please contact the Sandbar and ask for Jace. He'll get you in touch with your property."

He read it over a couple of times, then removed the description and added at the bottom: "You'll need to describe the thumb drive to take possession."

Mason felt better about that. He felt at least, he was doing something. He clicked, post, and watched as it uploaded. Then the message popped on his screen. Posted.

He walked out to the bartender and said, "If anybody calls here about a thumb drive, patch him through to Jace or me. Margo exited from the bathroom her eyes were still red. She caught up to him. "Is there any news?"

"No. But we're making some progress."

"Oh, Mason, I'm so worried."

He hugged his boss's wife, his girlfriend's sister, and his friend. He said, "I know. I'm worried too, Margo."

She stepped back and sniffed. "She likes you so much."

He grinned. "I like her too. More than I ever dreamed I could like anybody. More than I ever dreamed I would want someone in my life. It's unreal and then this. But I'm more determined than ever to find her."

"Thank you. Thank you. I'm trying to stay out here because I feel like I'm in the way. I don't know what to do. I don't know if I should go to the house and see..."

Mason froze, "Wait a minute. I'm just gonna run out to the house and make sure she's not there. That they're not holding her there."

"Don't go alone, take someone with you."

"I'll take Mitch with me."

Mason hustled back to the office. "Mitch, let's go out to Carley's house and make sure they didn't take her there."

"Will do." They rushed out to Mason's truck and hopped in. He drove them quickly toward Carley's house.

Mitch inhaled. "I doubt that they would take her there, it would be the obvious place to look, and they think police have already been there."

"That's true, but at least I feel like I'm doing something."

"Well, there is that."

As Mason sped to Carley's house, Mitch's phone rang again. "DeMario."

"This is Trey Fielding from Blossom Springs PD. We just got word that Jonathan Roberts out on County Road AA found a woman who had been kidnapped. We have units on the way."

Mason slammed on the brakes just before turning on Golden Acres Road, where Carley lived, and made the left to stay on Hospital Road. About two miles past the hospital, he took a left on County Road AA.

33

Carley fell to the ground; the sharp pain caused her to lose her breath. She heard the truck slam on the brakes, and another shot rang out. Another shot and sirens. Tears streamed from her eyes, and she struggled to breathe. She gasped, and foam came out of her mouth.

Panic spread through her body. She saw Mason's blurry face. He was so handsome. He yelled something. She didn't understand what he was saying, and he was floating away. She tried to ask him to stay with her, but he was so far away now. She couldn't hear him anymore and that made her sadder than anything. Mason.

※

Carley woke to the sound of a monitor beeping and something that sounded like air whooshing in and out. It was so annoying. It kept going and she wanted to go back to sleep.

She felt as if she were floating. She heard voices speaking in hushed tones. It smelled like medicine. Her stomach growled and she tried to move her hand over her stomach, but it felt like lead.

The heartbeat went faster, and the whooshing air did, too. She felt panic. She was tied to a bed, and she couldn't move. They found her.

She called out, "No!"

Strong hands rested on her shoulders, and Mason's deep voice whispered, "You're safe, honey. I'm here. You're safe."

"Safe," she said. It hurt to talk. It hurt to breathe. "Hurts."

"I know. It will for a little while, honey. You had surgery. But you're going to be just fine."

"Surgery."

Nothing made sense to her. She was running, then sharp pain and she fell to the ground.

She whispered, "I fell down."

"Yes. You fell."

She swallowed. "Water."

"You can have some ice chips, but no water just yet."

She heard the clinking of ice dropping into a cup.

"I'm going to raise the head of your bed a bit, so you don't choke on the ice."

She nodded but didn't say anything.

The soft buzz of a motor and the feeling of floating up. The floating stopped and it felt as if someone sat next to her.

"Can you open your eyes, Carley?"

She tried opening her eyes, but they felt as if they had weights on them. "Can't."

He chuckled. "Try again for me."

She swallowed and tried again. She managed to open her left eye slightly. She tried again, and both of them opened. She saw Mason sitting next to her, she was on a bed. Her heartbeat sped up, and Mason smiled the sweetest smile. "You're safe, honey."

She nodded and he held a cup to her lips. "Just a chip." An ice chip dropped into her mouth. "Swirl it around to wet your mouth."

The smooth, ice chip felt so good in her mouth. It was small and melted quickly. "More."

He grinned and gave her another ice chip.

She swirled it around the same as the other and felt a small amount of cold liquid slide down her throat. She followed the path of that cold liquid until it warmed and disappeared.

A door opened, and she heard Margo gasp. "Oh my, God, you're awake." She rushed to the bed and looked down at her. Carley tried to smile. "Hi."

"Hi. Oh, Carley. We were so worried about you."

Her beautiful sister's eyes filled with tears that then slid down her cheeks. "Don't cry."

Margo pulled a tissue from a box and dabbed at her eyes. "I can't help it. I've been crying most of the day."

Carley closed her eyes again. "Sleepy."

Mason's voice soothed her. "Go ahead and sleep. I'll be right here when you wake up."

***

Carley woke. Her eyes focused. The room was dark and so quiet. She listened intently and heard the heartbeat and air whooshing again. She heard something else, too. Taking a deep breath, she turned her head to see Mason reclined back in a chair that looked far too small to be comfortable, and his breathing was deep and steady. His right hand lay across his stomach, and his left hand rested on the arm of the chair. He was handsome in sleep. Peaceful and serene.

She looked around the room and realized, fully at least, she was in the hospital. She inhaled, felt a stabbing pain, and grunted.

Mason woke and sat up. His eyes focused on her. "Are you alright?"

She swallowed. "I tried to take a deep breath. It hurt."

He came and sat gently on the bed next to her hip. "Yes. You had surgery."

"Surgery."

"Honey, you were shot. The bullet entered from the back and lodged in the apex of your right lung. You had surgery to remove the bullet and patch you up. You'll be sore for a while."

"My throat is so sore."

Mason reached for the cup of ice chips and held it to her lips. "You can have ice chips for now."

She took a chip and swirled it in her mouth. "Your throat is sore because they inserted a tube to help you breathe until they repaired your lung. They also had to suck blood out of your chest cavity and lungs so you don't have further complications."

She nodded slowly. She lifted her right hand and laid it over her chest. It was bandaged up. She stared at the bandages for a moment, then rested her head back.

"Do you remember how you got that injury?"

She took shallow breaths and tried not to panic that it hurt to take a normal breath. He was here if she needed anything. He'd help her. There was no reason to panic. Not anymore. "Yes. They tied me to a bed with a zip tie." She spoke slowly and waited until her breathing could catch up. I sawed back and forth to break or tear the tie."

His jaw tightened. She saw the muscle in his cheek move as he processed what she'd said.

He took her left hand between his hands and stared into her eyes. "I'm so sorry."

"It's not your fault."

"It is. I was late. Jace stopped me to talk. Then Ethan called. I should have been there."

"Don't. Please."

She focused on breathing regularly so it wouldn't hurt. He stopped apologizing and they stared into each other's eyes for a long time.

She smiled. "Time?"

He glanced at his watch. "Eleven."

"Night?"

He smiled softly. "Yeah. You've been in surgery and then out of it most of the afternoon and evening. By design. They wanted your stitches to have a bit of time before being worked."

She nodded.

"Go back to sleep beautiful. I'll be right here."

She looked past him at the chair. "Not comfortable."

He grinned. "When I was in Afghanistan, this would have been called heaven."

She shook her head and opened her mouth, but he shook his head. "I'm fine. You need to heal so we can sleep in a bed together. Deal?"

She smiled and nodded. "Deal."

34

Mason drove slowly to Carley's house. He was finally bringing her home. It had been a long week.

He glanced at her briefly and she grinned. "I'm fine."

He nodded. "I know." He turned onto her road. "I can look if I want to."

She nodded and smiled. He couldn't wait to hear her laugh again. She'd need to be stronger for that though. Her therapy was going well, but she needed to keep going for a while. He'd make sure she did.

He turned into her driveway, the garage door was open, and Margo's vehicle was parked to the far right of the drive. He drove in past Margo's vehicle and parked.

He didn't need to say it, but he did. "I'll come around and get you."

She smiled. "Thank you."

He hurried around Carley's vehicle. He'd used her SUV because she would have struggled getting into his truck. He opened the door and held his hand out in case she needed to hold on to him. She knew just how to slide off the seat and not twist or bend to cause pain, as too much movement still took her breath away. Her lung function was great, considering what had happened. But it wasn't one hundred percent yet.

After moving herself out of the vehicle, she took hold of his arm, and they moved forward together. Margo flung the door open wide and had the biggest smile on her face. "Welcome home."

Carley smiled but didn't say anything. She needed her breath for movement. Once inside he asked, "Where do you want to go?"

"Living room."

He turned toward the living room. Jace was in the kitchen, and he grinned. "I'll go get the stuff from the car."

"Thanks," Mason responded.

He stopped at the sofa, and Carley slowly lowered herself onto it. He pulled the small pillow from the armchair and tucked it behind her lower back, so her wound didn't rest against the sofa.

Margo bustled in and sat on the coffee table in front of Carley. "I've made lunch. Turkey and wild rice soup. Let me know when you"re ready. The house is clean; laundry is done. I've been filling in at your office, so you haven't missed a beat."

Mason grinned and let the two sisters chat. He went out to the garage to help Jace carry in the plethora of flowers and gifts that had been sent to the hospital for Carley. Her room there looked incredible with all the flowers. All the nurses commented on the beauty of her room, and she gave a couple of her favorite nurses the flowers they commented on. She was generous, as well as all the other things he loved about her.

He stopped quickly as that thought ran through his head, and Jace looked up at him. "You, okay?"

"Yeah."

"You sure?"

"Yeah."

Jace stared at him a moment then pulled another floral arrangement from the back end of the SUV. "Jace, when did you know you were in love with Margo?"

Jace chuckled. "Ahh. I see." He handed Mason the flowers in his hand. "I don't recall a day. I only knew one day I didn't want to live without her."

Mason nodded and carried the flowers into the house. Jace was close behind him. They made several trips back and forth. The house resembled a funeral home, and he didn't care for it. It would be up to Carley to decide what to do with all of the flowers, as many were beginning to wilt anyway.

Margo bustled into the kitchen. "Are you men ready to eat? Carley thinks she's ready for some soup."

Jace patted his stomach. "I can eat. I love your soup, so count me in." He kissed her lips, and she giggled.

It was nice watching them together and Mason realized he wanted that too. He'd never had those thoughts before. He'd never met anyone he wanted to spend every day with.

He went to the living room and helped Carley up from the sofa. She'd learned how to use her legs, but having his arm to steady her was a bonus. He was also happy to oblige.

"Thank you," she said.

He grinned. "Any time."

She chuckled as they moved into the dining room. "It's beautiful," Carley said to Margo.

"Thanks, honey."

Margo acted like it was nothing, but she'd been here

most of yesterday and all morning, cooking, cleaning, and prepping for Carley's homecoming.

Margo carried the pot of soup to the table and set it in the middle. "I can dish if you'll hand me your bowl."

Carley held her bowl up. "Smells delicious."

Margo's smile was huge. They looked similar in so many ways and their smiles were one of them. When they genuinely smiled, and it reached their eyes, their resemblance was clearest. He and Jace were fortunate men. They'd found beautiful, fun, smart and self-sufficient women.

They ate their soup in silence. Margo had made fresh bread and an apple pie for dessert. He was genuinely stuffed.

His phone rang and he pushed his chair away from the table. "I'm sorry. excuse me."

He moved into the living room as he answered. "Hi, Mitch."

"Hi, Mason. I heard Carley went home today."

"Yes, we got back here about an hour ago."

"Nice. She'll heal faster there than anywhere."

"I think so too. What's up?"

"I just wanted to let you know that Ethan updated me about Layton Terry and Dustin Carter."

"Okay."

Jace entered the living room and watched him. "Hang on, Mitch."

He looked at Jace. "Would you all like to hear this update?"

"Yes."

His eyes moved to Carley's. She was watching him and nodded.

He swallowed. "I'm going to put you on speaker so Carley, Jace, and Margo can also hear this."

"Sounds good. Hello, Carley, and welcome home."

She smiled. "Thanks."

Mitch continued. "So I wanted to update you on Layton Terry and Dustin Carter. As you already know, Layton Terry died as a result of gunshot wounds the day after the shooting. Dustin Carter healed from his wounds and was on his way to a military prison; I can't disclose which one, but that transport was attacked, and he was murdered."

Mason nodded. "No shit!"

Mitch responded. "They were involved in selling hundreds of military secrets to Russia, Iran, and China. In total, they'd amassed millions of dollars trading these secrets to the highest bidders. None of those countries would want them making deals and giving away their contacts. We don't know which country got to Carter, but we're looking into it."

Mason shook his head. "Were Terry and Carter military?"

"Yes."

Mason's eyes darted to Jace's. Jace's jaw tightened. "Traitors."

Mitch continued. "Yes. Traitors."

Mason swallowed. "Are there more of them?"

Mitch let out a long breath. "Ethan and his crew are looking into it. For security reasons, I'm not able to divulge more than this."

"Of course. We appreciate knowing Carley doesn't have to look over her shoulder anymore. Thank you for the update."

"You're welcome. Carley, I hope you return to one hundred percent in no time. Listen to Mason; he's a phenomenal doctor."

He looked into Carley's eyes, and she smiled. "I know. Thank you."

35

Carley woke wrapped in the cocoon of Mason's arms. It felt so good to feel safe and comfortable. He'd taken care of her during her stay at the hospital. He dumbed down the doctor lingo for her, and step-by-step, he explained what to expect and why some of the therapies she had to do were important.

He'd been with her every day since she'd returned home a week ago. She'd gotten her stitches removed yesterday, and overall, she was feeling pretty good. She would be in therapy for three months in total. Her doctors, including Mason, felt she'd be able to graduate from therapy by that point. She practiced her breathing every day; Mason made sure of it.

She slowly rolled over to face him. When she turned, his eyes were open, and he stared into her eyes. A sleepy grin appeared on his face. "Morning."

"Morning," she replied, then kissed his lips softly.

"How do you feel this morning?"

She smiled. "Actually, pretty good."

A grin spread his lips and she couldn't look away if she

wanted to. He was seriously that handsome. Especially with bed-tousled hair.

"How good?"

She chuckled. Her hand slid down his chest, across his abdomen, and down until his thick hard cock was in her hand. His eyes stared into hers as her hand smoothed up and down his length. Pre-cum formed at the tip, and she smoothed it over the sensitive head of his cock. His breathing increased in speed as she worked him. His eyes closed, and she knew he was completely immersed in the feelings of her touching him.

He slid his hand down her back to her butt. He squeezed a cheek, then pulled her leg up and over his hip.

She grinned, as they hadn't had sex like this yet. She loved all these firsts. She positioned his cock at her entrance, and he slowly pushed himself into her.

She sighed. "Damn, you feel so good."

He grunted slightly. "You feel better."

He moved himself in and out of her. His speed increased as he grew closer to orgasm. He reached between them and pressed his thumb against her clit, then made small circles until her body shook, and she cried out his name as she was swept over the edge. Mason's sigh was sexy, and when he reached his orgasm, his groan was sexier. She held him close as they both let their breathing settle.

After a few minutes, his gruff voice whispered near her ear. "Are you alright?"

She chuckled and slipped her hand into his hair. "Yes."

His lips made small kisses from her shoulder, to her neck, up her jaw, and over to her ear. She sighed as he lavished kisses on her.

His arms wrapped around her tighter, and he held her close to his body for a long time. She massaged his scalp slowly with her right hand, as they relaxed with each other. His firm body felt perfect against hers. His warmth seeped into her bones and his caring and love could be felt.

She closed her eyes. He hadn't told her he loved her. She hadn't told him yet either, but she could feel something. She kissed his ear. "I hate to move, but I have to go."

His muscles relaxed and he unwrapped his arms from around her. "I'll get coffee ready for us."

"Thank you."

She slid herself to the side of the bed and slowly raised herself up. She let out a breath as she sat up straight and scooted to the edge of the bed. She padded to the bathroom, knowing full well Mason was watching her bare ass as she walked. Unfortunately, he also saw the bandage on her back where she'd been shot.

She shook her head as she thought about that. Not many people in the world could say they'd been shot. That was a good thing. Unfortunately, she had and it was honestly something she'd never, ever thought about before.

After she finished peeing, she washed her hands and dressed in a pair of light shorts and a loose T-shirt. Their routine had been to sit on the patio each morning and stare out at the gardens. She liked that routine and hated thinking about Mason going home.

Moving at a steady pace down the hall, she saw Mason already sitting on the patio, sipping coffee from his favorite cup. It was an older cup she'd had when she moved here. All it said on it was, "Badass". He said it summed her up completely.

Grinning she stepped outside and sat in the chaise next to him. He had her cup of coffee on the table between them. He had a plate of cookies on the table also.

"We still have cookies from Hanna?"

He chuckled. "We'll have cookies from Hanna for about a year. She sent over a ton of baked goods."

Carley giggled. "She's a good person."

He nodded and sipped his coffee.

She sipped her coffee, ate a cookie, and took in as deep a breath as she could.

"Are you getting anxious to go home?"

He turned his handsome face toward hers. His eyes searched hers for a bit and she saw him swallow. "'Not really."

"What about work? When do you have to go back?"

He took a giant breath, set his feet on the ground, and turned to face her. He leaned his elbows on his knees; his coffee cup was held between both of his hands, making the cup look impossibly small.

"I wanted to talk to you about that."

Her heart began to beat faster. She wouldn't have another boyfriend who didn't want to work. He seemed in no hurry to work right now, and her stomach tightened.

"So, your surgeon, Doctor Borders, has been calling me. At first, it was to offer a courteous update on your progress. By the third day you were in the hospital, he asked me if I was interested in getting back into the medical field."

His eyes met hers. "At first, I said I didn't think so, but he pointed out a few things he was impressed with. He said I was so good at explaining to you the things he said about physical therapy, your condition, and basic medical jargon. I told him I knew patients were so stressed when doctors explained things, but they didn't understand what that meant. Usually, they hate to ask and feel stupid, so they worry."

She swallowed. "You are very good at that."

He grinned but said nothing.

She sat up and put her feet on the patio across from his. She sat as he did, with her elbows on her knees and her cup in her hands. "You said at first."

He nodded. "You're good at that. Remembering things."

She chuckled. "Right. Now you think you want to get back into medicine?"

"They've offered me a unique position at the hospital here. It would be more consultative in nature and include follow-up. I wouldn't have to perform surgery if I didn't want to. I'm not sure I'm ready for that, but they would be open to it if I change my mind."

She set her cup on the table next to the cookies. Her heart raced and her stomach twisted. He seemed distant and sad. "Why does this seem like you're letting me down easy?"

His eyes jumped to hers instantly and he shook his head. "I'm not." He set his coffee cup on the table next to hers. He took her hands in his and stared into her eyes for a long time. "I'm not letting you down easy. I hope I'm not letting you down at all. However, I am interested in exploring this position. It would mean leaving the Sandbar, though. And Jace has been good to me."

She squeezed his hands and stared into his eyes. She loved his eyes. They were the most beautiful brown. "Jace will tell you he wants the best for you. He will also understand your decision."

He swallowed, then took another deep breath. "I don't want to let you down either."

She chuckled. "How is this letting me down?"

He swallowed again. "What if I can't do it?"

"You ask Jace for your job back, you see a counselor and we'll chat about it."

"It makes me look weak."

"It makes you look strong. Trying to step back into something you know you love, no matter what demons you battle, is the bravest thing anyone can do. You know the struggles you had in the past, but you're willing to go back and try again."

"Counseling is a requirement according to Dr. Borders."

"I think that's a great idea." She squeezed his hands again. "Why is Dr. Borders so interested in you? I mean besides the fact that he likes your bedside manner."

Mason chuckled. "Paramedics told them how I saved you when you were shot."

Her brows shot up in the air. "You saved me?"

He nodded slowly. "Your lung was filling with fluid, and you were coughing up blood. You couldn't breathe. I had to insert a tube into your chest to drain the blood until we could get you to the hospital." He pointed to the spot on her chest where she now had a small scar that would likely disappear in the months ahead. "I still carried a medical kit in my truck. You were running toward my truck when you were shot. It was Mitch DeMario who shot Layton Terry. He'd shot you, and Mitch saw him ready to shoot again. You fell to the ground, and instinct took over. I grabbed my medical bag, and without thinking, I did what was needed."

She cocked her head and the flood of memories rushed back to her. She saw his face. She heard words she didn't understand. Then his face disappeared. She couldn't breathe. "I remember bits and pieces of you there. When I finally regained consciousness, I thought I'd dreamed you up."

His right hand framed her cheek and his thumb brushed across her face softly. "I thought I was going to lose you. I worked as fast as I ever had and it was perfect. Perfect procedure. I saw you and knew I wasn't going to let you die. No matter what, you were going to live."

A tear slipped from her eye. "Thank you."

His thumb brushed it away. "I haven't had a nightmare since then. Isn't that weird?"

"No. I'm not a psychologist, but it seemed that you were haunted by patients of the past. I was a patient and you wanted to save more than anything, and you did."

"But I wanted all those other patients to live too."

"Of course, you did, but they weren't meant to live, or they were too badly damaged. It wasn't your skill or lack of it; it was the situation at hand and..." She shrugged her shoulders. "God's will."

He huffed out a breath. "Why would God make people die?"

"He didn't make them die, evil did. There are lessons in things. Some are horrible things like those patients you lost, but some are wonderful things like the birth of a child or the badly injured patient you save. If you were not on your learning journey, we wouldn't have met."

He leaned forward and kissed her lips softly. "I love you, Carley Page."

Her heartbeat increased, and the tears flowed once more. "I love you, Dr. Mason Thompson." She kissed him softly but chuckled. "But, for the record. I also love bartender Mason Thompson and his Sandbar Punch."

Mason laughed. "That's not my recipe."

She laughed, "It doesn't matter. I love the way you serve it."

He chuckled. "So back to your very first question this morning. Am I getting anxious to go home?"

She sat up straighter and waited for him to respond. He grinned. "I'd like to move again."

"Move?"

"Here. I'd like to move here and live with you."

A huge smile appeared on her face. She could feel her skin stretch. "Well, I was going to get a dog."

"I can sit on your lap."

She laughed. "I'd love for you to move here, but I get to sell your condo...again."

He nodded. "Actually, you can do that, but I already have a buyer."

"You do?" She took his hands in hers, "who?"

"Mitch. He's decided he'd like to move here and set up a security business in Blossom Springs."

"Oh wow. That's fantastic."

He laughed. He half stood and picked her up as if she weighed nothing, then set her on his lap. "It is fantastic. He's a great guy and we could use more like him here."

She wrapped her arms around his neck and kissed his temple. "My life feels complete right now."

He twisted and scooted them back so he could recline with her on his lap. She nestled between his legs and rested her back against his chest. His arms wrapped around her into the best cocoon ever. She closed her eyes and sighed deeply. "I'd still like a puppy though."

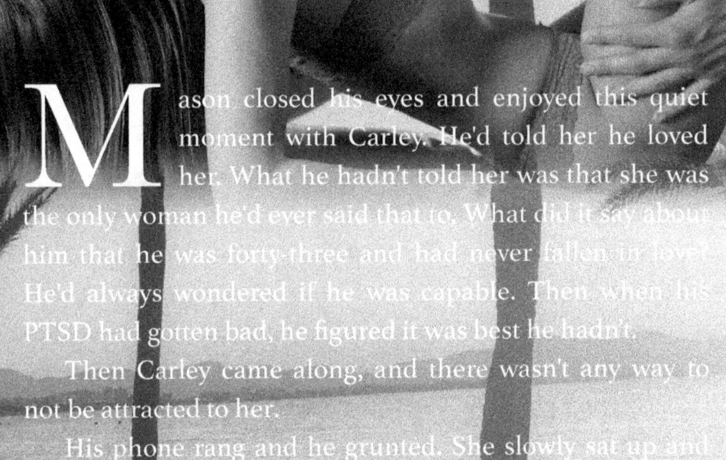

36

Mason closed his eyes and enjoyed this quiet moment with Carley. He'd told her he loved her. What he hadn't told her was that she was the only woman he'd ever said that to. What did it say about him that he was forty-three and had never fallen in love? He'd always wondered if he was capable. Then when his PTSD had gotten bad, he figured it was best he hadn't.

Then Carley came along, and there wasn't any way to not be attracted to her.

His phone rang and he grunted. She slowly sat up and he reached into the pocket of his shorts and retrieved his phone.

Glancing at the readout on his screen his stomach twisted slightly. He tapped the answer call icon. "Hey, Jace."

"Hi, Mason. I thought I'd let you know that Blossom Springs PD just called. They picked up the man who wanted the medallion."

Mason lay back against the chaise once more. Carley slowly turned and watched his face.

"Hang on. I'll put you on speaker so Carley can hear you."

He tapped the speaker icon and stared into Carley's eyes. "Go ahead, Jace. Carley's here."

"Morning, Carley. I just told Mason the police caught the man who wanted the medallion."

"Oh, my God," Carley whispered. "I'd completely forgotten about him."

Mason's leg itched where Isak Voss' bullet had finally stopped its journey. He scratched lightly as Jace spoke.

Jace chuckled. "There's been a lot going on."

Carley's eyes dropped to his hand rubbing his thigh and she grinned. She asked, "So what's the story with the medallion?"

Jace chuckled. "It appears the medallion is his. He's sort of homeless and wandering. He was watching workers at the Barracks and would sneak in before they finished at night. He'd slept in Mason's closet the night before you found the medallion. He woke and left the building when he heard workers coming in to work on the other units. The medallion was something his father held dear to him, and he carried it. It's about the only possession he has to his name."

Carley nodded. "I remember fluffing the carpeting up before Mason got there and wondered what had pressed it down."

Mason took in a deep breath. How many close calls had this gorgeous woman had recently?

"Mystery solved," Jace responded.

Mason took a deep breath. "Jace, are you going to be around today? I'd like to chat with you."

Jace hesitated a moment, then said, "We'll be here all day."

"I'll be there in about an hour."

"See you then, bud."

Carley grinned. "See you later, Jace."

The call ended and Carley grinned at him. "You saw his name on your phone and groaned."

"I like him...very much. I guess I've been feeling guilty about the hospital and having to make a decision. He gave me a chance when he didn't have to."

Carley leaned forward and kissed his lips. "That's what Jace does. He gives veterans a chance."

She turned so she faced him. She was the most beautiful woman he had ever seen. Sitting here in the sunshine, her facing him, and the sun glinting off her long dark hair, she looked like an angel with the light behind her.

She picked up his hands in hers. "I'd like to ask a favor."

His brows shot up in his hair. "A favor."

She laughed. "I know you've practically given up your life the past two weeks to care for me, but I have one more favor. I'd like you to consider working with Jace, Sid, and Quinn at the Legion counseling veterans. No one knows more than you what PTSD can do. If you are serious and will work with a counselor, you'll have someone helping you while you help others."

He watched her face. She was serious and so insightful. She was most likely right. He nodded. "I'll talk to Jace about it when I go in and chat with him this morning."

"I'd like to go with you if you don't mind."

"Really?"

"Yes. I need to get out of the house. It's not far and it won't be too taxing. I can also see Margo."

"I'd never deny you any of that. As soon as you need to come back and rest, you'll let me know. Promise?"

She laughed. "Yes, I promise."

"Okay. Then let's go get ready. I'll buy you breakfast at Hanna's, then we'll go to the Sandbar."

"Thank you."

He helped her up, then he grabbed their coffee cups and let Carley hold his arm as they entered the house. She didn't need to hold his arm, but at this point she liked it. At least he hoped that was it.

Setting the cups in the sink and the plate on the counter, they moved to the bedroom together. He made the bed while she pulled clothing from her closet and started the shower.

He heard her enter the shower and he pulled his phone from his pocket. He dialed his high school friend, Bear. His stomach twisted a bit and he stepped from the bedroom and into the guest room.

"Hey there, Sad Sack. How are you?"

Mason laughed. "I haven't been called Sad Sack in a long time, so I thought I'd call you to hear it."

Bear laughed. "Happy to oblige. What's up?"

"Well, I'm actually calling for the call!"

"No shit? Are you serious?"

"I am. Never been more serious in my entire life."

"Well, shit. It's about fucking time. I haven't made any money on you at all. A couple of the guys I've made money on twice."

"I only want to give you money once."

Bear laughed. "Okay, give me the deets."

37

Carley felt great today. Better than she'd felt in a long time. It was three weeks ago today that she'd been kidnapped and shot. It was still an event she couldn't believe she lived through. An event she hoped one day she'd forget. She was going into the office for the first time since that day.

Checking her outfit in the mirror, she was pleased with her appearance. The dark circles that had been under her eyes were gone. She managed a straight posture now, and she looked healthy. If a person didn't know her, they'd never know what had happened.

Mason stepped into the bedroom and whistled. "Sexy momma."

She laughed. "Thank you for always being my confidence booster."

He came to stand behind her and grinned in the mirror at the two of them together. His voice was low when he whispered, "Look at me with the most beautiful woman in the world. How did I get so lucky?"

She leaned her head back to rest on his chest and smiled

at him in the mirror. "I honestly believe I'm the luckiest woman in the world. However, I'm a little worried about those nurses at the hospital fawning over you."

He laughed. "You have nothing to worry about. I'm off-limits, and I couldn't be happier about it."

She cocked her head to the side. "Maybe I need to get you a ring to wear on your left hand so they can see it."

He grinned. "That's not a bad idea."

She planted that thought in the back of her mind for later. Today she had to see how long she could make it at the office. She stood straight and turned to face Mason.

He kissed her lips and then stared into her eyes. "Are you ready?"

"Yes."

"What do you do if you have to go see a home?"

"Mason..."

"What do you do? Humor me."

"I call Margo and you and leave the time, address, and the person's name. I also leave it in the computer. Addison will call me every fifteen minutes to check in."

Mason grinned. "Good. What are homeowners to do when you have a showing at their homes?"

"They are to stay there, out of the way, but present in case something happens."

He nodded. "And what if you're at the condos?"

"I need to let either Mitch or Quinn know what time the showing is and don't go in until one of them is there."

"Good." He turned and held his arm out for her to precede him from the room. She knew as she walked down the hall in their home he was watching her ass. She liked that. She watched his every chance she got. He had an amazing ass.

In the kitchen, she poured them each a cup of coffee. He

sat on a stool at the counter, and she stood across from him. "Can I make you something to eat?"

"No thanks. I guess they're having breakfast for me at the hospital as a welcome thing."

"Okay. Don't they normally do lunches?"

He shrugged. "I guess this way, the night shift can join in before they go home. It'll be easier for me to meet most of them."

"Oh. That's a great idea."

He grinned and sipped his coffee. "You'll be home at two today?"

"Yes. I promise. I can't wait to see what kind of surprise you have for me. And, once again, for the record, I think it's mean that you told me about it, and then you make me wait an entire day to see what it is."

He chuckled. "It's part of the fun. I'll say this, you'll be thrilled."

She smiled at her handsome boyfriend playing games with her. Then he said, "I think."

"Mason Thompson!"

He laughed. Looking at his watch he stood. "I have to go. I don't want to be late on my first day at the hospital. That wouldn't look good at all."

"No, it wouldn't."

He walked around the counter and wrapped her in a warm, snug, beautiful hug. His hands pulled her close, his right hand held the back of her head to his chest, and she closed her eyes.

The beating of his heart was comforting. Strong and sure. She smiled as she listened to it then took a deep settling breath. This is where she belonged. With this man. Right here in his arms.

She tried pulling away, but he held her close. "Just a minute more," he whispered.

She wrapped her arms around his waist and squeezed him tightly. She lifted her head and looked up into his eyes. "It's okay, Mason."

"We haven't been apart for three weeks. I'm...not ready. I'm worried. I want you safe."

She smiled, slid her hands up his chest, and cupped his face. "I'm safe. I'll be safe. I'll be very careful with every single thing I do. I'll text you often, but don't respond unless you can. I'll only text to let you know I'm safe, so you don't worry. I'll see you right here at home, our home, at two o'clock."

"Yeah. I like all of that." He bent down and kissed her once more. "I love you."

She smiled. "I love you too, and I'll never tire of hearing it from you."

He chuckled, stepped back, and nodded. He stared at her once more, then stepped out of the kitchen and into the garage.

She gathered their dirty coffee cups and washed them. She wiped down the counter and stared at the garage door. She hadn't been completely honest with him. She was scared shitless today. She had to leave the house for the first time by herself and she didn't know if she'd be able to do it.

She took a few deep breaths, then nodded. She grabbed her purse and her computer from the counter and strode to the garage door without thinking about it anymore. She could do this. She had to, she just had to.

38

Taking a deep breath, Mason opened the door to his truck when his phone buzzed. He glanced down at a text from Carley.

"I made it to the office! Go me."

He chuckled and texted her back.

"Good for you. I made it to the hospital."

"Look at us go!"

A smiley face then another text.

"Have a fantastic day."

"You too, beautiful."

He climbed from his truck and strode to the front door of the hospital. As he stepped inside, Dr. Walker Borders stood at the opening with a grin on his face. "Welcome, Mason. I'm thrilled you're here."

Dr. Borders held his hand out and Mason gripped it tightly and shook. "Thank you. I'm happy to be here."

Dr. Borders turned. "Follow me and I'll show you to your office and introduce you to your nursing staff."

After that, the day was a whirlwind of meeting people, shaking hands, learning computer systems, hospital procedures, and where everything was located. He found himself in the wrong department twice, and this was a small hospital. Everyone was friendly and pointed him in the right direction. Carley texted regularly, wishing him well. She was safe, she loved him and she couldn't wait to see him.

He couldn't wait to see her. She was hopefully going to love her surprise.

By one-thirty, he sauntered out to his truck, eager to see Carley and happy he'd made the decision to go back to medicine. The smells didn't seem to bother him anymore, not all of them anyway. A couple of times, he'd whiffed the anesthesia gases in passing, and that made his stomach turn a bit.

He climbed into his truck and tapped the phone button on his steering wheel to call Bear. The phone rang only twice, and he pulled from his parking space and headed toward home.

"Hey, there. I've been waiting for your call."

Mason chuckled. "Yeah. I'm headed home."

"I'm on my way."

"Are we all good?"

"Yep. All good."

"Great. See you soon." He navigated the fork in the road to the right to head home, a smile on his face. Hopefully, this was the right thing to do.

His stomach twisted a bit as he second-guessed himself all day, but Bear pulled in behind him in the driveway, and there was no changing his mind now. Carley wasn't home yet, which was good. He wanted a bit of time to set up her surprise.

Pulling into the garage, he waited as Bear hopped from his SUV. Mason met him by his vehicle and shook his hand. "Nice to see you, buddy, how are you?"

They hugged and Bear chuckled. "I'm doing well. I've been excited all day for this."

"Not as excited as I've been."

"Are you nervous?"

Mason took a deep breath. "Yes, and then again, no. It's been a roller coaster of emotions today. It was my first day at work and Carley's first day back to work. We've been through a lot the past few weeks."

"Yeah, you sure have. I've been reading some of the newspaper articles about it. Both of you shot on the same day in separate incidents. What the ever-loving hell, man?"

Mason nodded. "It can't get much weirder than that."

Bear shook his head. "Well, let's get set up."

"I have everything in the truck. Help me carry it all in."

Mason and Bear set up Carley's surprise. He was ecstatic and hoped she'd be as well.

Bear stood. "Okay, I'm out of here. Documentation is in the folder here." He handed the folder over. "Keep in touch and I want to know all about it later today."

Mason chuckled. "I'll let you know."

Bear glanced down at Carley's gifts and shook his head. "She's a lucky woman."

Mason's cheeks heated and he shook his head. "I'm the lucky one. Honestly."

Bear slapped him on the back and Mason chuckled.

He closed the garage door behind Bear, then hurried to the bedroom to change his clothes. Just as he pulled his shirt over his head, the garage door opened. She was right on time.

He sauntered out to the kitchen and waited for Carley to walk into the house. The instant she stepped inside, he handed her a glass of champagne. "Congratulations on your first day back."

"Oh, that's so sweet." Before they tapped their glasses together, she said, "Here's to your first day of work, Dr. Thompson."

He chuckled and they tapped their glasses and took a sip of their champagne. He kissed her lips, softly at first, then deeper. He'd have been happy to continue, but there were other things to shower her with.

He stepped back and took her hand. "Follow me."

She giggled. "I've been so excited all day."

He chuckled. "Me too."

He led her to the sofa. "Take a seat, please."

"Okay."

She settled into the sofa, still moving stiffly so as not to cause pain. She sat and stared up into his eyes, a huge smile on her face. He stared a moment. "I always want you as happy as you are right now."

"I want you happy too."

He grinned. "Stay right where you are. I'll be right back."

He exited the living room and stepped into the first bedroom to the right of the hallway. He opened the kennel door and a little fur ball bounded out of her kennel and out the door. Luckily, she turned in the right direction and Mason followed her as quickly as he could.

Carley stared at him a smile still on her face, not seeing the little bundle on the floor. He pointed down and her mouth fell open.

"A puppy!"

Mason grinned. "She's a purebred German Shepherd."

"Ohh...Mason." She slid from the sofa to the floor and the little ball of fur ran to her and climbed in her lap. Mason knelt down in front of them, laughing as Carley laughed. The puppy jumped and licked at Carley's face, her hands, and her legs. She climbed in her lap and tried climbing up her torso. She was a bundle of energy. He hoped this wasn't a mistake.

"Oh, Mason this is fantastic. I'd thought about it, but...I had no idea you'd gotten one."

"Well, I have a friend who is a breeder. He brought her down today."

"Oh, my God. She's simply adorable."

Mason laughed. "She sure is."

Carley scratched the puppy's back and tried getting her to settle long enough to really look at her. Mason's stomach was a ball of knots as he waited for the perfect moment to finish his surprise.

Finally, the pup settled slightly, and Carley looked at the tag on her red collar. "Read it out loud," he said.

She started reading it. "Will you marry..." Her breath caught and her eyes darted to his. He was on bended knee as he stared at her. "Will you marry us?"

She swallowed and tears flowed instantly down her cheeks. "Mason..."

He held a ring in his hand and swallowed. "Will you marry me, Carley Page?"

"Yes." She sniffed. "Yes, I'll marry you. Absolutely, I'll marry you!"

EPILOGUE - CARLEY

Carley woke and smiled. Today, she'd marry her man. She texted as she smiled.

She got out of bed, opened Heidi's kennel, and followed her down the hall to the back door.

Heidi did her business as Carley poured herself a cup of coffee and then poured fresh food into Heidi's bowl. She opened the back door to let Heidi in and scratched her behind her ears. "You're such a good girl."

As Heidi excitedly ate her breakfast, Carley jumped in the shower.

She exited the shower and applied lotion to her legs. Reaching for her panties, Heidi grabbed them from the stool in the bathroom and took off running.

"Heidi, no!"

The mischievous little pup kept running through the

bedroom. She lay on the carpet and began chewing on Carley's panties.

Slowly, Carley moved toward Heidi to snatch her panties back. Just before she could reach her though, Heidi took off at a run and out the door. Carley's panties were on a stroll.

"Dammit," she huffed.

She was the only one home, so she took off down the hall, naked as the day she was born, in search of her pup and her panties. Heidi stopped in the kitchen and dropped the panties near her water bowl as she sloshed water around while she drank. She was a messy drinker and Carley's panties were paying the price.

Carley tried crooning to her. "Hey, pretty girl, are you thirsty from being naughty?"

Stepping closer, Carley bent to retrieve her panties, but Heidi had other ideas. She grabbed the panties with her dripping-wet mouth and took off running. Carley stopped and waited for her to stop.

Making her way to the cabinet where Heidi's treats were stored, she opened the canister of treats and pulled one out.

Heidi was such a smart girl and very food-motivated, and she knew that was her treat cabinet and container. She dropped the panties and ran into the kitchen, sliding on the floor and crashing into Carley's leg. Carley handed her the treat, and at the same time, she bent and scooped Heidi into her arms.

She'd grown so quickly these past few months. Now at four months old, Heidi was full-bodied and heavy. Carley carried her to her kennel and placed her inside.

"So much for your freedom you little imp. You'll have to stay in here until I'm ready to go."

Latching the kennel closed she went in search of her

panties. She found the wet, wadded panties in a sad lump near the fireplace in the living room.

Holding them up, Carley's shoulders dropped. These were her special panties for her wedding day. She inhaled deeply and assessed the damage. Sloppy, wet, torn lace on the right leg, and the pretty little silk bow was gone. Hopefully, Heidi didn't eat it.

Checking the time on her watch, Carley sauntered into the laundry room and tossed the panties into the washing machine, added a laundry pod, tossed in a towel so it wasn't being totally wasteful, and started the machine. Then she moved back to the bedroom, put on a different pair of panties until hers were washed and dried, then put on her pretty lacy bra. The one that matched her ripped panties. Then, she wrapped herself in a silk robe while she did her hair.

She turned her blow dryer on and began blowing out her hair. She'd pulled out her old electric curlers for this special occasion. She'd practiced several times this week with them and liked the style she managed versus her curling iron. She wrapped her dark hair around the curlers, snapped on the clips to hold them in place, and began pulling out her makeup.

Heidi came bounding into the bathroom and Carley stopped in place. Her heartbeat increased and her breathing was stilted. "Mason? Are you home?"

He wasn't supposed to see her before the wedding. She slowly stepped out of her bathroom. Mason wasn't in the bedroom. Her throat went dry, and her stomach twisted. This wasn't funny. Not after what she'd been through. She called out louder. "Mason!"

Her fingers began shaking. She tiptoed to her closet and

pulled out the pistol Mason had insisted she have and practice with. They practiced every week.

She loaded the magazine into the stock, turned off the safety, and moved back out to the bedroom. The entire time, Heidi bounced around her feet, thinking this was a fun game.

Carley moved into the hallway, holding her gun pointed to the ceiling until she saw the threat. Her heart pounded so hard in her chest that she feared she'd pass out. Heidi ran past her down the hall and back to the kitchen. Heidi's lapping at her water bowl reached Carley's ears, but no other sound could be heard.

Carley neared the second bedroom and slowly stepped inside, keeping her back to the wall. She glanced around the room, opened the closet, and jumped back, pointing her pistol into the void.

She got brave and looked under the bed. No one was there.

Taking in a deep breath, she stepped into the hall and checked the third bedroom. Heidi bounded in and ran to the far side of the bed. Her tail wagged furiously, and Carley's stomach twisted. She took a deep breath and reminded herself to stay calm. What a stupid thing to say to herself. She was anything but calm. She peered over the side of the bed and saw Heidi playing with the big rope toy they'd gotten her.

Letting her breath out she moved out to the living room, from this vantage point she could see into the kitchen and the dining room. There was no one here. Shaking her head she decided she must not have closed Heidi's kennel door all the way. Heidi came to her, and Carley bent down and patted her pooch softly. "Okay, little lady, in you go."

Heidi obeyed and Carley fastened the kennel latch,

ensuring she had it latched properly. The washer stopped spinning and she pulled her panties from inside and tossed them in the dryer. She moved back to the bedroom to begin applying her makeup. For good measure, she closed and locked the bedroom door, then sauntered to the bathroom, laying her pistol on the counter. Just in case.

Once her makeup was applied, she pulled the cooled curlers from her hair. Her phone rang and she tapped the icon to answer it, seeing her sister Margo's number on the readout.

"Good morning."

Margo laughed. "Good morning. What time are you arriving?"

"Soon. I have my hair almost done, and my makeup is on. Heidi has been mischievous this morning and chewed my panties and slobbered them up, so I had to wash them. As soon as they dry, I'll be over."

"Okay. I'll have breakfast ready in thirty minutes."

"You're cooking?"

Margo laughed. "No, when I say, 'I'll have breakfast ready...' I mean, Jace will have it ready. I'm busy trying to get my baby sisters' butts in gear."

Carley laughed. "That's why I stayed here last night. I knew they'd be up talking all night, and I have a big day."

"I know you do, honey. Put your panties on and get over here."

She laughed. "I'll see you soon."

She ended the call sand pulled out the shorts and t-shirt she'd wear to Margo's. They'd dress in the Governor's Mansion after breakfast, then a limousine Mason hired would carry she and her sisters to the Sandbar, where she would marry her lover. She couldn't wait.

Dressing quickly, she put her gun in the gun safe, locked

it up, and stepped from the bedroom into the hall when Heidi ran up to her as if they were meeting for the first time.

"Heidi!"

Carley looked down the hallway and didn't see anyone again. She took a few steps toward the kitchen, and Heidi bounded down the hall before her. Carley swallowed the lump in her throat and took a deep breath. She watched her pup's behavior and didn't see anything different. Heidi always alerted her to a stranger.

She moved to Heidi's kennel once more and smiled at her pup. "Go to bed."

Heidi trotted to her kennel and lay down inside. Carley locked it up, then moved to the kitchen to wait. And watch.

Heidi, who was incredibly smart, lay like a perfect little lady and watched her in the kitchen. Carley grinned, opened the treat cabinet, and pulled a treat from the jar. Heidi grew restless and began crying. Carley lay the treat on the floor where Heidi could see it. Heidi stared for a while, then Carley stepped back and watched. Heidi reached her paw through the slats in the kennel and pushed the latch up. Then she wiggled it over, using her paw and her nose until the door popped open. She ran to the treat, and Carley shook her head. "You are too smart for me, girl."

EPILOGUE - MASON

Mason woke in Quinn's spare bedroom excited for today. He grabbed his phone from the nightstand and looked at it. Carley's text awaited him, and he smiled reading her morning message. He replied,

> "Good morning. I'm excited to see you, and for the record, I don't like sleeping alone."

He sent it off, got up and used the toilet, then jumped in the shower.

He missed his woman and his pup. Heidi had wormed her way into both of their hearts within minutes of being in their home. It was uncanny how much he loved her. But, as with any pup, she required constant attention. If she wasn't looking for a place to pee, she was chewing on something she shouldn't or getting into things. Any basket, bag, or bundle on the floor was fair game. As she grew, it was harder to keep things from her. Plus, she was smart!

He stepped from his room at the Kurtz's home and smelled coffee. As he entered the kitchen, Quinn sat at the

table reading the paper, with a steaming cup of coffee in front of him.

"Morning," he said.

Mason grinned. "Morning."

Quinn started to rise but Mason held his hand out, "Don't get up. I can manage."

He saw the cup sitting next to the pot and poured himself a cup of coffee. Cream and sugar were there if he needed it. He didn't.

He sat across from Quinn at the table and took a deep breath. Quinn set his paper down and grinned. "Are you excited?"

"I am."

"You're a good pair."

Mason laughed. "I think so too."

Quinn grinned. "Hanna's already at the bakery. I have to leave in about an hour, to help her load the van, and deliver to the Sandbar."

"Thank you both so much for all you have done for us. I'll make the bed before I leave."

"No, you won't. You're our guest, and we'll take care of it. You worry about the things you have to do today."

"Thank you. I guess my job today is to pick up the flowers at the Flower Shoppe and get them to the Sandbar. Apparently, they have several events today, and our delivery would have been cutting it close. I volunteered, so Carley didn't panic."

"Good idea."

Mason finished his coffee and stood. He rinsed his cup in the sink and shook Quinn's hand. "Thank you for letting me stay last night. It was both a superstition and a test. Carley wanted to know if she could do it. She's trying to face her fears, per her counselor. She did fantastic."

Quinn laughed and nodded. "She's strong. I'm glad she's getting better. How about you?"

"I haven't had a nightmare since Carley's incident. I'm seeing my counselor regularly. I'm functioning in a hospital, which I wouldn't even go into previously. Life is good."

Quinn grinned at him. "I'm happy for you. Also, thank you again for helping us at the Legion. You're a natural."

"Honestly, it's helping me too."

"It does do that. It helps all of us."

Mason moved toward the bedroom. It was time to get moving toward his wedding. He quickly packed his duffel bag; his wedding suit was at Margo and Jace's. Jace was bringing it today to the Sandbar. They'd opted for a beach wedding, just like their friends before them. They'd say their nuptials on the second-floor deck, facing the water so they had the most beautiful view of the water and the horizon. It had become their peaceful place when they needed a night away from Heidi's shenanigans. It felt natural to marry there.

He stepped out to the garage, where Quinn had already opened the door and was putting his suit in the back of his truck.

Mason grinned. "I'll see you in a bit."

"Looking forward to it," Quinn answered.

Mason climbed in his truck and headed toward the Flower Shoppe. He pulled into the jam-packed parking lot. "Wow, busy day," he muttered.

He sauntered into the Flower Shoppe to see its owner, Izzy Payton, directing deliveries to various areas of the shop. She looked up to see him, and a huge smile spread across her face.

"Mason, I'm happier to see you right now than anyone else in the world."

His brows shot up. "Wow, that's nice."

Izzy laughed. "Don't get a big head. I need your flowers out of here, so I have room for some of these deliveries."

He laughed. "Okay. Understood. Point me where I need to go."

"Come this way." She led him to a back room and a table with a sign on it that read, *Page/Thompson Wedding*. "These are all yours." She looked around and saw a young man, likely around seventeen years old, entering the back of the greenhouse area. "Robert, please help Mason load these flowers."

"Okay," he called out.

Izzy turned to Mason and grinned. "Congratulations on your special day. Please don't be offended that I have to bounce off. It's nuts here today."

Mason laughed. "No offense. Bounce off at will."

She didn't linger. She was gone in the blink of an eye, but the boy named Robert had taken her place. "If you want to move your vehicle around the building and to that door over there..." He pointed to the right. "I'll start moving the flowers to the door for ease of loading."

"Great. I'll be right around."

Mason moved through the inside of the shop, dodging people as they carried various items to the register or browsed the shop. He quickly moved his truck, and within a matter of minutes, he and Robert had his truck loaded, and he was on his way to the Sandbar. The day was going smooth so far.

Arriving at the Sandbar, Grace Hoffman and Hanna Kurtz were setting out baked goods as Quinn carried them from Hanna's delivery van.

Grace looked up to see him. "Oh, thank goodness you're

here. It'll take a bit to decorate with the flowers. I'll help you unload."

He and Grace made quick work of unloading, then she shushed him off to get dressed in the back. He'd already worked up a sweat, as the weather was humid and growing warmer by the minute. Jace waited for him in the office. "Good morning. I've fed your bride and her sisters. My house is a mass of giggling and chatting, and I needed to get out."

Mason laughed. "I bet. Thanks for feeding her."

"She didn't eat much, but she told us a hilarious story about your pup stealing her panties this morning. Sounds like you both have your hands full with that one."

He grinned. "We do, but after she matures a bit, she's going to be wonderful. We start puppy-training classes next week."

Jace shook his head. "That is not for me."

Mason chuckled. "There are days it isn't for me either, but I've fallen hard for that little shit."

Jace stood. "That's why God makes them cute. Sucker!"

Chuckling he took a deep breath. "I think I need to hose off again, moving all the flowers sweated me up."

"Yeah, I've been sweating in the kitchen helping Marco get today's meal prepped. Let me show you what Margo and I have added to the back room."

He followed Jace out of the office and around the corner. Jace unlocked a door and flipped on a light. "We added this a few weeks ago. I get so sweated up sometimes, and if I have to serve or tend bar, I don't want to smell. Now, I can come back here and hose off."

Mason stepped into a small but nice bathroom. The tile floor looked like wood, and the shower was made of glass and ceramic tiles. The sink and toilet gleamed. "It's fantastic."

"Well, Margo likes the best of everything, but she's also a fantastic negotiator. It didn't cost us what it would have otherwise. So, I let her do her thing. Anyway, jump in the shower, there's a soap dispenser in the corner. When you're finished, I'll take mine...again."

Wasn't that perfect? Mason hurried through his second shower of the day and dressed in his suit. He exited the bathroom and took the elevator upstairs to see how the decorating was coming along. A quick glance at his watch, and he counted down the minutes. Only ninety to go.

The Moment You've Been Waiting For!

You've followed their journey through love, loss, and triumph—now it's time for the *ultimate celebration!* Mason and Carley are tying the knot, and their wedding is everything you've dreamed of and more.

But this isn't just a walk down the aisle... Secrets are revealed, unexpected guests arrive, and emotions run high as this unforgettable day unfolds. Can Mason and Carley overcome the last-minute hurdles to finally say *"I do"*?

PLUS: Don't miss the bonus epilogue that gives you a heartwarming glimpse into their future—because every love story deserves a happily-ever-after.

Get your exclusive access to this special chapter now! Celebrate love, laughter, and happily-ever-afters with Mason and Carley.

https://www.pjfiala.com/sensual-nights-bonus-epilogue/

ENJOY THIS BOOK? YOU CAN MAKE A BIG DIFFERENCE

Your Review Matters!

As an independent author, I don't have the big budgets of major publishers for splashy ads or subway posters (not yet, anyway 😌). But what I do have is something far more valuable—amazing readers like you.

Your honest review is one of the most powerful ways to help my books reach other readers. If you enjoyed this story, taking just a few minutes to share your thoughts would mean the world to me. Reviews, even short ones, make a huge difference.

Click below to leave your review and help others discover *Seductive Nights*:

➡️ https://geni.us/SensualAll

Thank you for your support—it means everything! 🩶

ALSO BY PJ FIALA

I'm fortunate to be able to do what I love. It's a blessing.

My list of written works has gotten so long I needed to move it to my website! How's that for blessed?

Anyway, click the link below to see the list of all of my books.

Thank you so much for reading.

https://www.pjfiala.com/bibliography-pj-fiala/

or scan the QR Code below.

MEET PJ

About the Author

Writing has always been my dream, but it wasn't until I found the courage to put pen to paper that my life changed in the most profound way. Creating stories that resonate with readers and bringing to life flawed yet lovable characters brings me endless joy—and I hope my books bring you the same.

When I'm not writing, you'll likely find me enjoying time with my family or hitting the open road with my husband, Gene. We're avid bikers who love exploring new destinations, meeting fascinating people, and soaking in the beauty of this incredible country.

Coming from a proud family of veterans—including my grandfather, father, brother, two sons, and daughter-in-law—I have a deep appreciation for service and the sacrifices that protect our freedoms. Their dedication inspires me every day, and I'm honored to share stories that celebrate resilience, love, and the American spirit.

My online home is https://www.pjfiala.com.
You can connect with me on Facebook at https://www.facebook.com/PJFialaı,

and
Instagram at https://www.Instagram.com/PJFiala.
If you prefer to email, go ahead, I'll respond - pjfiala@
pjfiala.com.

COPYRIGHT

Copyright © 2024 by PJ Fiala

All rights reserved. This book or any portion thereof may not be reproduced or used in any manner whatsoever without the express written permission of the publisher except for the use of brief quotations in a book review.

Publisher's note: This is a work of fiction. Names, characters, places, and incidents either are the product of the author's imagination or are used fictitiously. Any resemblance to actual events, locales, or persons, living or dead, is entirely coincidental.

Printed in the United States of America
First published 2025
Fiala, PJ
SENSUAL NIGHTS / PJ Fiala
p. cm.
1. Romance—Fiction. 2. Romance—Suspense. 3. Romance - Military
I. Title – SENSUAL NIGHTS
ISBN-13: 978-1-959386-88-9